KU-024-879

THE TWELVE-MONTH MARRIAGE DEAL

BY
MARGARET MAYO

MILLS & BOON®

All the characters in this book have no existence outside the imagination of the author, and have no relation whatsoever to anyone bearing the same name or names. They are not even distantly inspired by any individual known or unknown to the author, and all the incidents are pure invention.

All Rights Reserved including the right of reproduction in whole or in part in any form. This edition is published by arrangement with Harlequin Enterprises II BV/S.à.r.l. The text of this publication or any part thereof may not be reproduced or transmitted in any form or by any means, electronic or mechanical, including photocopying, recording, storage in an information retrieval system, or otherwise, without the written permission of the publisher.

® and TM are trademarks owned and used by the trademark owner and/or its licensee. Trademarks marked with ® are registered with the United Kingdom Patent Office and/or the Office for Harmonisation in the Internal Market and in other countries.

First published in Great Britain 2009
Harlequin Mills & Boon Limited,
Eton House, 18-24 Paradise Road, Richmond, Surrey TW9 1SR

© Margaret Mayo 2009

ISBN: 978 0 263 20864 1

CAVAN COUNTY LIBRARY
ACC No C/243769
CLASS No F
INVOICE NO 8340 Book Nest
PRICE €12.54

Set in Times Roman 10½ on 12 pt
07-1009-47761

Harlequin Mills & Boon policy is to use papers that are natural, renewable and recyclable products and made from wood grown in sustainable forests. The logging and manufacturing process conform to the legal environmental regulations of the country of origin.

Printed and bound in Great Britain
by CPI Antony Rowe, Chippenham, Wiltshire

Cavan County Library
Withdrawn Stock

Elena wanted to back away, but it was impossible. All she could do was watch in fatal fascination as his face got closer and closer. Study the intent in his beautiful grey eyes framed by decadently thick lashes. Observe that his breathing got just that little bit faster. And his lips—his beautifully moulded lips—were opening the merest fraction.

There was not a thing she could do but await her fate. But at the same time she ordered herself not to respond, not to let him see by the simplest of movements that pressure was building up inside her, threatening to spill over the second his mouth claimed hers.

Was it disappointment she felt when he didn't kiss her straight away? When he cupped her face in his hands, his thumbs stroking her expectant lips, his touch so gentle it was like the brush of a butterfly's wing and yet as deadly as snake's venom?

Elena couldn't keep her promise to herself. Her resolve flew out of the window, her lips parting freely, the tip of her tongue coming out to moisten her lips and encourage Vidal's touch, her head rocking back on her shoulders. It was wrong, all wrong, but somehow she couldn't help it.

Margaret Mayo was reading Mills & Boon® romances long before she began to write them. In fact she never had any plans to become a writer. After an idea for a short story popped into her head she was thrilled when it turned into a full-scale novel. Now, over twenty-five years later, she is still happily writing and says she has no intention of stopping.

She lives with her husband Ken in a rural part of Staffordshire, England. She has two children: Adrian, who now lives in America, and Tina. Margaret's hobbies are reading, photography, and more recently watercolour painting, which she says has honed her observational skills and is a definite advantage when it comes to writing.

THE
TWELVE-MONTH
MARRIAGE DEAL

CAVAN COUNTY LIBRARY

CHAPTER ONE

'YOUR'RE expecting *me* to *marry* Vidal Marquez?'

Elena looked at her parents as though they were out of their minds. This was the last thing she had expected when they had asked her to come home. The very last thing. She didn't know what she *had* been expecting, but it certainly had never entered her head that they would try to persuade her to marry Vidal.

Her already huge brown eyes widened into enormous orbs of shock and doubt and her heart began an unsteady tattoo. It was actually unbelievable; it was insanity of the highest order. How could they ask this of her? How could they even *think* it?

It was her sister who had been going to marry Vidal. They'd been engaged for months. And now her sister had run away! And no one knew where she was. So what had happened? And more to the point, why were they suggesting she take her place? Why was it so important?

None of it made any sense.

The afternoon sun streamed through the window, adding highlights to her glossy black hair. It was ironic that it was such a gorgeous day outside and yet here in her parents' house her whole world was slowly falling apart.

'It's ludicrous.' She stood tall and proud, her beautiful face flushed with fury and indignation, her golden eyes almost shooting sparks of fire. Her hair, cut just below her ears with a side fringe, swirled in complete disarray every time she shook her head. 'For one thing I do not plan to get married for a very long time. I have a business to run, in case you're forgetting. I've spent years getting where I am today and I have no intention of giving it up to marry—' she drew in a deep, unsteady breath at the enormity of what her parents were asking '—my sister's *ex*-fiancé.'

Elena deliberately put great emphasis on the word *ex*. She loved her parents dearly, but for the life of her she couldn't understand why they were suggesting she take Reina's place. Plenty of couples split up and there was never a thought of their siblings stepping in.

Actually it was hard to believe that Reina had done this. Her elder sister never put a foot wrong. She herself was the wilful one, the one who her parents sometimes despaired of. When she'd gone to live in Los Angeles they had feared for her well-being. And yet she was running a successful wedding-planner business while her sister had turned her back on the wedding of the year.

She could imagine how hard they had taken the news, Vidal's family too. The wedding was already in the planning stages. Anyone who was of any note in Spain would already be on the guest list.

'I'm sorry Reina's putting you through this,' she said, privately thinking that it was better her sister had found out now that she didn't love Vidal rather than after their marriage, 'but is this about losing face? Why would you even *think* about me taking her place? Why can't the merger go ahead without a marriage between the families?'

'Because,' answered her father quietly, 'we fear that without it the deal will be off. We didn't tell you this before,' he added unhappily, 'but—it was an arranged marriage—for business reasons. We all thought that Reina was happy with the situation. We thought she actually loved Vidal, but—' He lifted his shoulders and let them fall again, his face a picture of sadness and sorrow and fear for the future.

'Arranged?' Elena could not believe what she was hearing. The whole situation was getting more bizarre by the second. 'No wonder Reina ran away. What were you thinking? And now you expect *me* to take her place. No way! Not ever! I don't even like Vidal! If you want my opinion he's a pompous, arrogant bas—'

'Elena!' Her father's shocked voice resounded through the room. 'I will not have that language in my house.'

'Nevertheless it's what he is,' she declared firmly. God, she was seething. This was her worst nightmare. How could they even *think* about asking her to marry this—this…? Words failed her.

She had never understood why they wanted to merge the two banks anyway. Not that she'd ever had any inclination to work in the business; she'd opted for freedom. She loved her parents dearly, but sometimes found their affection stifling.

'There is another reason,' said her father, his arm

about her mother's shoulders now, putting on a united front, 'and I hate having to tell you this, but—' he dragged in a deeply troubled breath '—the bank is in trouble. We fear that we shall be financially ruined if Vidal doesn't take over.'

Looking at him, Elena saw the deep lines of strain on his face and the worry in his eyes that she had assumed were because of her sister's actions, but it now appeared that something more serious was afoot. Even her mother's face was filled with fear, her brown eyes haunted, sunk more deeply than Elena had ever seen them.

Instantly, Elena folded her in her arms, holding her trembling body close. Her mother had always been such a strong woman that it hurt to see her like this.

Her parents' bank was a private one, whereas Vidal dealt in corporate banking. Theirs wouldn't be the first one in trouble that he had bought. They were talking about a merger, but Elena knew very well that if Vidal got his hands on it, it would be the end of the road for them. All she could hope was that he was offering them a fair deal. Though why she had to become a part of it Elena had no idea.

'So,' said her father firmly a few seconds later, 'you will do this? It's not only for ourselves, you understand, but our employees too. Some of them have been with us for a very long time. We owe them to do the best we can.'

Elena screwed her face up and shook her head. 'I can't, I'm sorry, but you're asking the impossible.' Surely they realised the absurdity of her marrying a man she did not love, a man she hadn't seen in years, a man who did nothing for her whatsoever?

What she could remember of Vidal Marquez was that he had always thought himself a cut above everyone else, even as a child. Therefore it went without saying that he would be unbearable to live with. No wonder Reina had got out while she could.

Her heart felt heavy when she saw her father's arms go round her mother as she almost collapsed. They were making this so very difficult. She loved them to death, didn't want to do anything to hurt them, but marrying a man she didn't even like was too big an ask.

When she saw that even her father, usually such a strong man, had tears in his eyes, she said quietly, 'Are you sure there isn't any other way of saving the bank?'

Her father shook his head. 'None at all.'

She closed her eyes and let her breath out on a deep sigh. 'I really don't want to do this,' she said quietly, 'but—I don't like seeing you two so worried either. I'll give it some serious thought. Though I'm not actually promising anything, you understand.'

Faint relief shone on their faces and they both put their arms around her.

Elena did not see how she could do as they asked, though. It would mean putting her whole life on hold, maybe even cancelling it altogether. She loved what she did and had thought when her mother called and said she was needed at home that it was to help plan her sister's wedding—not her own!

Tension reigned in the Valero household for the next few days. Elena hated seeing her parents' distress, but she hated even more the thought of marrying a man she did not love. There must be some other way to save the bank.

Vidal had always looked down his nose at her. There

was eight years' difference between them and as a child he had always considered her of no consequence. Vidal's younger brother, Fernan, was more her own age and he had been her constant companion, while Reina had been friends with Vidal. It was why she had not been surprised when their engagement had been announced. Never in her wildest dreams had she imagined that it was not a love match.

'You are coming tonight?' asked her father over breakfast on Saturday.

'To the charity dinner?'

He nodded. 'Your mother and I think it important that we go. We need to keep up appearances. We don't want anyone to know that we're in any kind of trouble.'

'Of course I'll come,' she said immediately. 'Will the Marquezes be there?'

'I imagine so,' said her father.

Her heart did a little hop, skip and a jump. It meant that Vidal would be there too. Was he aware that her parents were attempting to pair her up with him? And if so, what were his thoughts on the matter? She imagined that he would be as horrified as she was. Unless getting his hands on their bank was far more important than marrying for love. He'd done well for himself, she'd heard. His banking organisation was now the biggest in Spain. And she would face the man himself in just a few short hours.

Vidal could not take his eyes off the strikingly beautiful young woman who had just entered the room. Of its own accord his heart leapt and he instantly wanted to get to know her. She was tall, slim and very, very elegant, confident in the knowledge that she looked good.

Her short, dark hair revealed a long, slender neck around which a choker glistened with black gemstones. Her skin was soft and honeyed and he knew that he had to hold her, to touch, to feel—to enjoy!

Two thin straps that matched the necklace held up a black dress that moulded her body in such a way that each movement she made showed off the rounded curves of her breasts, each sway of her hips emphasised the pertness of her bottom.

He felt himself growing hard. This woman needed serious investigation.

She slowly circled the room, talking and laughing as she met people she knew—and was introduced to those she did not. She was vivacious and exciting, confident in her skin, walking with the grace of a female panther. He wondered if she had claws to match. There was something about her that was oddly familiar. Yet he could not recall ever having met her before.

'She's grown into quite a looker, hasn't she?'

Vidal turned and realised that his father had been watching her also.

'Who is she?'

'Why, Elena, of course. I'm surprised you didn't recognise her.'

Elena! Elena Valero! Surely not? 'I thought she lived in America?'

His father nodded. 'She does. She's home on a family visit.'

Now he knew who she was he could see the young

girl she had once been. But what a transformation. From gauche to graceful. From plain to sensationally, heart-stoppingly beautiful. From stick thin to enticingly slender with curves in all the right places.

Dios! His heart tapped out a rapid tattoo. She had turned into a magical creature who was in danger of sliding beneath his skin with the stealth of a viper. Reina had rarely spoken about her sister so he'd not really thought about her in all these years. Now she filled his mind and he couldn't wait for her to finish circling the room and reach his side.

Would she fail to recognise him? Or had he perhaps not changed as dramatically as she had? How many years had it been since he'd last seen her? Six since she went to America. But even before that he'd been too busy getting on with his life to take any notice of her. As far as he was concerned she'd been a wild child. Thoroughly spoilt, totally conceited, no interest in anything except herself.

He could not take his eyes off her, though, and suddenly she turned and looked at him, nothing more than a fleeting glance before she resumed her conversation. But it had been enough to heighten his desire even further.

Her eyes were enormous in her elfin face, but there had been no recognition. She'd felt him watching her, that was for sure, it had been a critical stare, but she had no idea who he was.

Nevertheless it felt like a lifetime before she reached his side. A lifetime in which he had enticed her into his bed, undressed her slowly, allowing his eyes to appreciate every inch of her amazing body before finally making crazy, fantastic love. Thank goodness she couldn't see his heart hammering like a mad thing within his chest.

'Vidal!' She held out her hand.

So she did know him! All this time she had known exactly who he was—giving her the advantage! And the cold glare she had sent in his direction had been condemning rather than curious. He was none too pleased at the thought. In fact, he was rather annoyed.

'Well, well, well, if the little girl hasn't grown up.'

Immediately the words were out he knew that it had been the wrong thing to say. He wanted to bed her, not offend her. But hell, he'd been caught off guard and it was not a feeling he was accustomed to.

Elena lifted her chin and glared, beautifully, her eyes, more gold than brown at this moment, exquisitely fierce. 'How many years has it been since we last saw each other?'

'Quite a few,' he admitted, wondering what it would really feel like to have this woman beneath him. Heavens, he hadn't felt like this since he was a teenager and in love for the first time. His body was infused with a heat that threatened to overcome him.

'Exactly,' she retorted sharply. 'You've changed, I've changed. Is it so remarkable?'

'I almost didn't recognise you.' He wasn't going to tell her that he had failed to do so. Oh, no. He had no intention of putting himself down in her eyes. 'May I be permitted to say that the transformation is sensational?'

He didn't let his eyes move from hers. Just listening to her voice caused an ache in his gut. It was soft and lilting, like the finest music. *Infierno*, this woman was sending threads of temptation through every fibre of his body. He had never met anyone who had ignited his fire so suddenly and so thoroughly.

'Thank you, kind sir.'

It was a mocking comeback and it didn't please him. 'I hear you're on a rare visit to your family.'

'Rare?' Her back stiffened and she stood just that little bit taller. 'Just because you and I haven't bumped into each other, doesn't mean that I don't come home often.'

'But not as often as you should.' Cold grey eyes looked into hers. 'What I'd like to know is why you felt the need to move to America in the first place. Doesn't life here satisfy you? According to your sister, your parents were heartbroken, and I can perfectly understand why. Maybe they didn't say anything to you. You saw it as an adventure, but they felt that you were turning your back on them.'

'How do you know what they felt? How dare you criticise me?' she shot back, her eyes hotter than ever. 'What I do is none of your business. I'd like to say it's been nice speaking to you, Vidal, but I'm afraid it hasn't. If you have nothing kind to say to me then it's best we don't speak at all.' And she began to walk away.

In an instant he caught her arm. 'Elena, we have a lot to catch up on.' His whole body went up in flames as he crushed her enticing body close to his, felt those long, sensuous limbs slide agonisingly against his more powerful ones, experienced the torment of her amazing breasts pressed into his chest.

'Do we?' she asked coldly. 'I don't blame my sister

for walking out on you. You're an arrogant swine who's poking his nose into something that doesn't concern him.' Tugging herself free, and with a final condemning glare, she marched away.

He had no choice but to let her go, not if he didn't want to create a scene. But his eyes followed her, watched the swing of her hips, the long graceful movement of her legs, half expecting her to glance back over her shoulder. She did not disappoint. And he met her eyes head on.

Such beautiful eyes, sloe shaped and a rich, dark golden-brown, fringed by long, thick, black lashes. There was a curious mixture of hauteur and interest in the way she looked at him and he allowed himself to smile faintly. Have no fear, Elena Benitez Valero, you'll never walk away from me again.

To think that he had almost married Reina!

The thought hit him hard as he got ready for bed later that night. He had not spoken to Elena again, but he had watched every movement she made, saw the ease with which she talked to almost everyone present, flirting outrageously with the young men sitting either side of her at the dinner table.

He had also noticed the way that she carefully avoided looking at him and was grimly amused. Perhaps it meant that she too had felt a spark ready to ignite? Could it be that beneath the arrogance she was Miss Fire and Brimstone? His body hardened at the thought of getting to know her—intimately. *Very* intimately.

When he had agreed to marry her elder sister it had merely been a convenient partnership to form the merger of their banks. Reina had been willing and no one except themselves, his brother and their parents had been aware that it was not a love match.

But recently Reina had begun to have doubts. She wanted a real marriage, she said, she wanted to fall in love and live the fairy-tale dream. So he had done the honourable thing and released her from their engagement. Naturally, for Reina's sake, he had let everyone believe that they had fallen out, and he had seen no reason why he should not still help her parents.

In fact, he had been ready to put things into motion—until tonight when he met Elena!

In an instant he'd had a dramatic change of heart. Elena would fit the bill as his wife perfectly. He had only to think of her delectable body, those fantastic breasts cupped in his hands, her incredibly long legs wrapped around him and those plump, delicious lips pressed hard against his, to know that he wouldn't be satisfied until he had her in his bed.

He had made up his mind.

No Elena, no merger.

He knew how worried her parents must be. They had no idea yet that he had been thinking of going ahead with the merger regardless of his marriage to Reina. Maybe this was the reason Elena was here. Maybe they were trying to persuade her to take her sister's place!

The thought brought a smile to his lips.

All he had to do now was sit back and wait.

Or maybe use a little light persuasion!

Elena wouldn't agree to it straight away, he was aware of that. She wouldn't worry whether her parents' bank prospered or sank. She had turned her back on them. Goodness knew what she got up to in America. He didn't know and he didn't care.

Regardless, she was a stunning woman now and all he wanted was her beside him—every night.

Vidal went to sleep with a smile on his face.

Having met with Vidal again Elena was even more convinced that marriage to him was out of the question. He had changed almost beyond recognition. Gone was the young man she remembered. This man oozed sophistication. It crept out of his pores like an unwanted drug. His thick, dark hair, which had always refused to be tamed, now sat sleekly on his well-moulded head. And his powerful body suggested hours spent in a gym.

His eyes hadn't changed; they were still a startling grey and actually rather attractive. It was his arrogance that really annoyed her. He might be the president of El Banco de Marquez, but his manners and his attitude towards her had certainly not improved.

She had known he was watching her across the room; she had felt his eyes on her the whole evening. It had sent cold shivers down her spine and a resurrection of the dislike she had felt for him when she was younger.

But what she hadn't expected was the way he had greeted her. Little girl indeed! Was that how he still saw her? Admittedly he had tempered his comment by saying she had grown up sensationally—but she guessed that was designed to make himself look good.

And his suggestion that she wasn't being fair on her parents had really got her back up. She rang them every day, for pity's sake, and visited as often as she could. They had never uttered one word of reproach and had always insisted that they were proud of her for making something of her life.

It was why she couldn't understand why they wanted her to give it up to marry Vidal.

What sort of a marriage would it be when he still treated her as Reina's baby sister? He would never accept that she had grown up, or that she was a success-ful businesswoman in her own right. She couldn't imagine anything worse than being married to him. He might have grown more handsome, staggeringly so. And he most definitely looked the part of one of the richest men in Spain. But as for anything else...

CHAPTER TWO

'I FEAR I'm wasting your time—as well as my own.' Elena's chin was high, her eyes fiercely defiant. Vidal had telephoned almost before she had got out of bed this morning and said that they needed to talk—so here they were in a tiny restaurant tucked away in the back streets of Seville having breakfast, and she had scared herself to death by feeling an unexpected and extremely scary response to him.

He wore a different cologne from last night, something light and musky and intensely sexy. And he looked as fresh as if he had had eight hours' sleep. Yet she knew he couldn't have had more than four. The dinner had gone on and on, with music to dance to if people wanted, although most had ignored it, preferring to catch up with each other instead.

Vidal had been one of the last to leave. As had she. There had been so many people she hadn't seen for years who had kept her talking.

And he had kept his eyes on her.

She had given no hint that she was aware of it, ignoring him completely, even slipping away before he could stop her to say goodnight.

For some insane reason this morning, though, from the instant she'd set eyes on him a fire had ignited inside her, flaring swiftly, burning fiercely, filling her with irrational feelings that set off a mild panic.

She told herself that it was angry resentment she felt, not a response to a magnificent body, and that she ought never to have accepted his invitation. What was the point when she had no intention of agreeing to the plan?

Actually she had no idea what Vidal's feelings were on the matter, so in one way it would be interesting to hear what he had to say. If he had an ounce of compassion in him surely he would go ahead with the so-called merger without marriage. They could then sort out the whole sorry affair and that would be an end to it.

'What makes you think that you are wasting my time?'

His voice was a rough, low growl, and the intent look in his eyes made her feel as though he were trying to hypnotise her. He had gorgeous eyes, sometimes grey, sometimes silver, depending on the light—or the mood he was in—with savagely thick lashes that could hide his feelings in a second.

'I cannot think of a nicer way to start the day,' he continued. 'As I said last night, Elena, you've grown up remarkably. You are now a confident, extremely beautiful, extremely elegant young lady.'

'Whom you almost didn't recognise,' she countered coolly. 'Whereas I had no trouble identifying you.'

'I am flattered,' he said, but although his voice sounded sincere she caught a flare of something else in his eyes. A look that said he was furious that she should have recognised him when he hadn't realised who she was.

'Don't think it's flattery,' she retorted. 'I would have had to be blind not to notice you watching me the entire evening. I'm curious, though, as to what was in your mind. Were you weighing me up, wondering whether I'd be a better proposition than my sister? Don't worry,' she added quickly when his dark brows rose question-ingly. 'My parents have told me what the position is. I imagine this is the reason I'm here now?'

Vidal held out his hands in open submission. 'Guilty as accused.'

'And do you really think I'll say yes?' He was out of his mind if he thought that. Entirely deranged. Not in a million years would she marry this man. She had no in-tention of getting married, not to anyone, not for a very long time. She'd gone out with guys in Los Angeles, but never seriously. She didn't have time, for one thing, it had been hard work building up her agency and now that she had made it she had no intention of letting any-thing—or anyone—get in the way.

'No, I don't,' he surprised her by saying. 'I can think of no woman who would agree to such a thing.'

Relief flooded through her, filling her body with a warm feeling of liberation, and she took a sip of her coffee. Vidal understood! She had done him an injus-tice! She smiled, and was just about to tell him how happy she was that he felt the same when his next words had her gasping in horror.

'Unless, of course, she thought that there was some-thing in it for herself?' His voice had gone an octave lower and he looked at her from beneath half-closed lashes.

Immediately Elena flashed her magnificent eyes.

'How dare you suggest such a thing? I need nothing from you—or indeed any man. I'm quite capable of supporting myself, thank you very much.' It hurt that he thought she was so mercenary and she would have liked nothing better than to slap his face hard.

'But you are going to be a dutiful daughter and help out your parents?'

'By marrying you?' she countered fiercely, jabbing a piece of toast with her knife. 'You're out of your mind if that's what you're thinking.'

'But you will!' he insisted.

His arrogant confidence angered Elena even further. 'I'm worried about my parents' future, naturally, but there has to be another way out of the situation. If you were half a man you would let the business deal go through without all this nonsense of uniting the banks by marriage. I was appalled when my mother told me that Reina's was an arranged marriage. I thought she loved you. I was happy for her. But I can honestly say that I don't blame her for leaving you. The marriage would never have worked, not without love. And neither would marriage to me work. At least you knew Reina. You and I are strangers.'

She felt like getting up and storming out, or at the very least throwing something at him. How could he accuse her of being mercenary? The man was seriously insane. But at least she now knew how much he wanted their bank. If he was prepared to marry her, a woman he'd never liked, never had time for, then he had to be desperate.

'We could have fun getting to know each other.' The words were dropped quietly into the air between them.

There was even a tiny smile curving the corners of his mouth.

'Fun?' Elena wanted to scream the word at him; it was hard keeping her voice level. 'How can you say that? How can you describe marriage between two people who dislike each other's guts fun?'

His smile widened. 'Perhaps we're each interpreting it differently?'

'Precisely,' she snapped. 'Mine is that it would be *hell*.' She deliberately put emphasis on the word and saw the sudden change in his eyes, quickly disguised. 'If you want to know what I think, Señor Marquez, I believe that you're prepared to do whatever it takes to get your hands on my parents' bank. Even if it means marriage to someone you—you despise.' Her breathing had deepened by the time she had finished and it was all she could do to sit still.

Vidal's face really did harden now. His eyes grew fiercely angry, his brows drawing together in a ferocious frown. 'So that is what you think of me? Let me tell you, something, Señorita Valero, if it were not for the fact that I do not wish to see your parents in trouble I would not be doing this. Do you think I want to marry someone like you? Someone who has turned her back on her family? When they could do with your support you have not been here. Tell me, what is it that you do over there in the States? If I remember rightly all you were ever interested in was having a good time.'

Elena could not believe she was hearing this, and especially from Vidal. He certainly wasn't doing anything to enamour her with him—in fact, he was driving her further and further away. She was tempted to get up and storm out of the restaurant, except that she did not want to give him the pleasure of seeing how much he had hurt her by his unkind comments.

'I don't have to tell you anything,' she snapped fiercely, her head held high, her eyes shooting sparks of fire. 'You can think what you like, but the fact remains that the thought of marrying a man I do not love fills me with horror. My parents are aware of this and I believe they are hoping that you will do the honourable thing and go through with the merger regardless.'

His eyes glinted shafts of steel and he sat up straighter in his chair, his body as taut as a bow string. 'Good try, Elena, but it is not to be. If you don't agree to marry me then the deal is off.'

Elena let out her breath on a deep sigh, feeling as though all the stuffing had been knocked out of her body. This was turning into a nightmare. 'What are you made of, Vidal? Certainly not flesh and blood. You don't have a compassionate bone in your body. You're cruel and mercenary and marriage to you would be sheer hell. Do you really think I'd be prepared to put myself through that?'

'I haven't got where I am today by being soft,' he growled, 'and I certainly don't intend to start now. You either marry me or your parents lose their business. It's as simple as that.'

Simple? How could he say it was simple? He was using emotional blackmail. He was trying to use her to get what he wanted. Reina had thwarted him so now it was her turn. Damn the man! If he thought she was going to change her mind then he was very much mistaken.

'You do not care who you hurt to get what you want, do you?' she demanded, her eyes fiercely aggressive. 'You'd marry someone you don't even like to further your massive ego, to pile more coffers into your bank. My God, I hate you.'

Vidal shrugged indifferently, his silver eyes ever watchful on her face. 'You're entitled to your opinion.'

It was as though her words had meant nothing, as though they had drained away like water off a duck's back. Hot, fierce anger pulsed and pounded inside her head. This man was unbelievable! 'You're not denying it?'

Vidal gave a tiny shrug, his lips pulling down at the corners. 'I think we should forget this entire conversation and finish our breakfast instead.'

He *was* denying it! Only good manners stopped Elena from getting up and walking out. And the thought that her parents would be devastated if she arrived home too soon, especially if she told them that Vidal Marquez was a swine and she wouldn't marry him if he were the last man on earth.

There had to be some other way of persuading him to go through with the deal. Maybe she ought not to have been so hot-headed? Maybe she ought to have been nice to him instead of getting his back up right from the beginning. She had played this all wrong. Taking a deep breath, she forced herself to calm down. 'I guess you're right, we should enjoy our food.'

But enjoy was not a word she could associate with eating in front of Vidal. She merely nibbled on her toast and drank copious amounts of coffee. Neither the merger nor marriage was mentioned again, they both did their best to be pleasant and amiable, but nevertheless their hostility simmered beneath the surface, waiting for one wrong word to bring it back to life.

It never happened. Polite to the end, Vidal took her home, suggesting as she got out of the car that they meet again the next day to discuss the matter more fully. 'I realise it was wrong of me to want to talk business over breakfast,' he said. 'Come to my office tomorrow and we can discuss matters there.'

Elena wanted to tell him to go to hell, that there was nothing left to talk about. Hadn't she made herself clear? But he had gone, his powerful car roaring away into the distance. She stood there watching until he had completely disappeared and then walked slowly into the house.

Her parents were waiting and she had to tell them that they hadn't yet reached a decision. She had never seen her mother look so disappointed and it was all she could do not to fling her arms around her and promise that she would find some other way to help them.

Not that there was a way. Even though her wedding-planner business was doing very nicely for itself she didn't have nearly enough resources for what they needed.

The following day Elena shivered as she dressed carefully for her further meeting with Vidal. She knew that she would need every inch of armour if she was to remain cool and positive so she wore a severely tailored black suit, teaming it with a cream shirt. A pair of stiletto heels gave her the height she needed to match up to Vidal's impressive stature and she was ready.

It was the end of the day and they were meeting in the bank's inner sanctum reserved for boardroom meetings. Deliberately she was a few minutes late. There was no way she wanted to be there first, tapping her fingers impatiently, trying to still her racing pulses while she waited for Vidal.

Instead he was the one doing the tapping. From outside the door she could hear his footsteps as he paced up and down, and she paused a moment or two listening.

Although she had intended remaining cool and calm, as she once again denied that marriage to him would work, Elena's heart rate increased. There was no disputing the fact that Vidal was one hell of a sexy man. Had the circumstances been any different she might have found herself actually fancying him. As things stood he was the most hateful man on earth. Nevertheless when she eventually turned the handle and entered the room she managed a neutral expression.

'I'd begun to think you weren't coming.' In contrast to the business suit that she wore he was in shirt-sleeves, rolled up to the elbow, revealing strong, sinewy forearms covered with fine, silky, black hairs. His jacket was on the back of a chair, suggesting that he had been here for some time. The collar of his shirt was undone, the knot on his tie loosened. Making her almost wish that she weren't so formally dressed.

Nevertheless she held her head high as she faced him across the boardroom table. 'I've not changed my mind.'

Clearly her forthrightness shocked him because his eyes grew instantly hard, his face developing harsh angles. 'So there's actually no point in you being here?'

He sighed. 'What do your parents think of your decision? Or have you not told them yet?'

Elena lifted her shoulders, pausing a moment before letting them drop again. 'I've said nothing. I thought we should talk again first. I thought we might come to a mutually satisfactory arrangement.' The moment the words left her lips and she saw the dangerous narrowing of Vidal's eyes, Elena knew that she was wasting her breath.

'Were you not listening yesterday when I said that it was marriage or nothing?' There was a glimmer of steel in his eyes now, his tall, powerful body silhouetted in front of the only window in the room. 'You're wasting my time, Elena. If that is all you have to say then I suggest you turn right round again and go.'

'And you're being unreasonable.' Elena knew that she had to make one last desperate attempt to change his mind. Unfortunately he was a man like no other and it dismayed her when a shiver of awareness ran down her spine. She wanted to avert her eyes—except that it would give him an advantage. Instead she looked boldly into his face, refusing to analyse the feelings that were creeping like an illness through her body.

'I would suggest that you look more closely at yourself, Elena,' he said softly, his voice all the more dangerous because of its quietness. 'I thought my offer was very reasonable.'

Elena shook her head angrily. 'You really think that agreeing to marry a man I do not even like is a practical solution?' What planet did he live on?

'It is if you want to help your parents.' His hard eyes

didn't leave her face. 'On the other hand why am I not surprised? You've done very little to help them so far.'

If the expanse of the table had not been between them Elena would have hit him. This was the third time he had insinuated that she didn't care about them. Her eyes blazed like molten gold. 'You know nothing, Vidal.' And her whole body grew rigid with anger. 'But I'll tell you this—somehow I'll find another way of getting them out of this mess, and it won't be with your help. I can think of nothing worse than tying myself to a man like you.'

With that she spun on her heel and marched out of the room.

He did not try to stop her.

As she walked away, Elena heard the telephone ring and Vidal's deep voice answering. The next second he called her name.

'Elena!' And then more urgently, '*Elena!* It is for you. It is your father.'

Elena felt her heart slam against her ribcage as she took the phone. There had to be something seriously amiss for him to be ringing her here. '*Papá*, what is wrong?'

'It is your mother,' he said. 'She is not well. I did not want to disturb you at this crucial time, but—'

'But what, *Papá*? What has happened to her?'

'She is in hospital, *mi querida*. She collapsed shortly after you left. I am sorry to have to tell you this now, but I am very worried about her and I thought that you—'

'You did right,' she breathed, feeling her heart panic. 'Are you with her?'

'*Sí.*'

'Then I will be there as soon as I can. Did they say what is the matter?'

'Not yet. They are doing tests.'

Vidal had been listening to her conversation and as soon as she handed the phone back to him he insisted on taking her to the hospital himself.

'I have my own car,' she protested.

'Maybe, but you are in no fit condition.'

Elena gave in reluctantly and sat quietly all the way to the hospital in the back of his chauffeur-driven limousine. Vidal held her hands tightly, trying to stem the trembling that would not stop. His hands were warm, but hers were icily cold. In fact, she felt cold all over.

'My mother's never ill,' she said as they pulled to a halt and she jumped out.

'I'm sure she'll be all right.' Vidal laced his arm protectively about her shoulders as she hurried along the hospital corridor and Elena did not even think about shrugging him away. She needed human contact; she needed every shred of comfort.

They met her father pacing one of the side rooms, unable to sit and wait for the news. There were tears in his eyes as he hugged Elena. 'I'm sorry I fetched you out of your meeting.'

'I'd have been cross if you hadn't,' she scolded with a faint smile. 'Have you heard anything yet? What happened? She was all right earlier.'

Her father nodded. 'I know, she was cooking dinner when she collapsed. I don't know what's wrong with her. How long are they going to be?' He glanced at his watch for what Elena guessed was the hundredth time in the last half an hour. 'No one tells you anything in this place.'

'I'll go and find out,' said Vidal firmly.

Elena was glad he was taking charge. Her father, usually a strong, capable man, looked broken. And so sad that she wanted to hold him in her arms and comfort him. But she knew that if she did they would both break down in tears and it wasn't what was wanted. They needed to be strong.

Before Vidal even made a move a doctor came to see them. 'Your wife's comfortable,' he said quietly to her father, 'but unfortunately we have discovered a heart murmur, which we believe has been made worse by stress. She told me that she has been under some considerable strain recently, but mentioned that she hopes it is about to be resolved. If so there will hopefully be no recurrence. But you do need to look after her, Señor Valero. No more worries, you understand?'

'Thank you,' he answered with a confirming nod. 'I will take care of her.'

When the doctor left the room, Elena hugged her father, tears spilling from her eyes. 'I had no idea *Mamá* had anything wrong with her. We must stop her from worrying so much.'

Her father looked from Elena to Vidal and back again. 'You are the one with that power, my child. Is it good news?'

CHAPTER THREE

VIDAL watched Elena's face as she struggled to answer her father's question. There had been times during their last two meetings when he had felt that he was in danger of bursting a blood vessel. Not only was she gorgeous to look at, but feisty too, and he loved that in a woman. Every hormone in his body jerked into life whenever they met and he wanted her with a desperation that was not good for his health.

Reina had been so different. Good-looking, yes, but he'd never felt for her what he was now feeling for Elena. He and Reina had not even slept together, although no one would ever have believed it. They had kept up the illusion of being very much in love.

'*Papá*, of course it is good news. I was on the verge of telling Vidal that I would marry him when you telephoned.' Elena turned, daring him to dispute it, fierce anger flaring in her eyes.

Vidal immediately smiled and pulled her to him, relieved that her father couldn't see her expression. Golden daggers of light shot across the space between them, blinding him, telling him that although she had agreed to the union in principle she had no intention of sharing his bed.

How naïve she was. Did she really believe that he would settle for anything less? She didn't know him very well if that was the case. It would be interesting persuading her to think differently. Even the thought of it sent a hot surge of desire through his loins. 'You have done the right thing,' he whispered in her ear. 'I knew all along that you'd see sense.'

Her eyes flashed more arrows of fury, but when she turned back to her father they had gone.

'Mi querida,' he said, enfolding her in his arms, 'you have made me so happy. Your mother, too, will be relieved. It will help her pull through this. She has been out of her mind with worry.'

'No more,' she told him quietly.

'You are a good daughter.'

Elena nodded, though Vidal was well aware of the conflict raging inside her.

'I am proud of you.'

'I am proud of her too,' Vidal said to her father, holding Elena against him. 'I have to admit that she took some persuading. Which I perfectly understand since she has her own life in America. But loving daughter that she is she put her parents' troubles first.' With slow deliberation he lowered his head and touched his lips to hers.

Elena stiffened, though Vidal gave no indication that he was aware of it, giving a satisfactory smile instead as he lifted his head, quelling the urgent feelings that had shot like lightning through his limbs. It was going to be a fight, persuading this lady to change her attitude towards him.

At least the first hurdle was over. There would be many more, he was aware of that. He was also aware that his life, which had become rather routine and unexciting of late, was about to be turned upside down.

And how he was going to enjoy it!

It was not until they left the hospital and were on their way back to the bank to collect her car that Elena allowed herself to give full vent to her feelings. 'Don't think that because my mother's health has forced me into agreeing to marry you that I'm happy about it.'

'I never thought for one moment that you would be,' came Vidal's calm reply. 'But I admire you for putting your parents first.'

'I had little choice,' she retorted.

'It occurs to me, Elena, that neither of us had any choice. Not if we want to help save your parents' bank.'

And was that really his concern? Elena wondered. Or was it the fact that he would be the one gaining? Another step towards total domination of the banking industry? 'Maybe,' she agreed. 'Nevertheless there are a few ground rules I wish to make.'

One black eyebrow rose. 'I hardly think you're in a position to talk rules, Elena.'

She ignored his comment, fixing her stormy golden eyes onto his silver ones. Her heart struggled to beat its regular rhythm. It felt like a dead weight in her chest, desperately wanting to resume normality, but knowing that it couldn't while her emotions ran so high.

Vidal's brows slid up, his expression reminding her that whatever she said it would make no difference. Vidal would do what Vidal wanted to do.

She took a deep breath and spoke. 'I need your assurance that this marriage will be in name only.'

'Oh, no, Elena.' It was instant denial, his steady eyes fixed firmly on hers. 'How could I possibly marry a woman as beautiful as you and not take you to bed? What you are suggesting would be sheer torture.'

He had her over a barrel and he knew it. Elena sat in stunned silence for several long minutes. 'I can't believe you're saying this. We hardly know each other. How can you—?'

'*Querida.*' His voice gentled and he slid an arm across her shoulders. 'We have known each other most of our lives. We played together as children.'

'No,' she protested, 'it was Fernan who was my friend, not you. You were too old for me. You looked down your nose at me.'

'But I noticed you.'

'And you used to tell me to run away. It's what I feel like doing now.' As far as she could possibly get. Back to America would be perfect.

'But you won't because of your mother's health.'

There was a light of triumph in his eyes and Elena felt like taking a swipe at him.

'Perhaps I should persuade you that it won't be as hard as you evidently think?' As he spoke, Vidal's arm tightened, his eyes not wavering from hers.

Elena felt as though she had been turned to stone. She wanted to back away, but it was impossible; all she could do was watch in fatal fascination. Watch as his face got closer and closer, so close that she could see the pores in his skin. Study the intent in his beautiful grey eyes framed by his decadently thick lashes.

Observe that his breathing got just that little bit faster. And his lips—his beautifully moulded lips—opening the merest fraction.

There was not a thing she could do but await her fate, while at the same time she ordered herself not to respond, not to let him see by the simplest of movements that pressure was building up inside her, threatening to spill over the second his mouth claimed hers.

Was it disappointment she felt when he didn't kiss her straight away? When Vidal cupped her face in his hands, his thumbs stroking her expectant lips instead, his touch so gentle it was like the brush of a butterfly's wing, and yet at the same time as deadly as snake's venom?

Elena couldn't keep her promise to herself. Her resolve flew out of the window, her lips parting freely, the tip of her tongue coming out to moisten her lips and encourage Vidal's touch, her head rocking back on her shoulders. It was wrong, all wrong, but somehow she couldn't help it.

Taking his cue from her, Vidal slowly lowered his head until his lips claimed hers. It was a defining moment and Elena now knew without a shadow of doubt that there was no way on this earth that she could live with him and not let him make love to her. For a reason she did not even try to fathom there had been an instant connection, one that she could not deny or refuse.

If she had to marry this man then why not make the most of it? It would be hell on earth if she didn't. He was the sort of man no woman could resist.

Her fate was sealed.

'I will, however, be prepared to wait until you are ready.'

Her eyes widened. As far as she was concerned it was an empty promise. Hadn't he just seen how easily she responded to him? No way would Vidal wait. He was a hot-blooded male who needed a woman.

'And—I'll tie you to the marriage for one year only. At the end of it you'll be free to walk away and carry on with your life as though it has never happened.'

Her eyebrows rose. 'How very noble of you.' And how easy he made it sound. One year wasn't very long. On the other hand she couldn't bear to think that she would be losing her freedom for twelve whole months. It sounded like for ever. In the normal run of things it would fly by, but married to Vidal, no matter that she found him gut-wrenchingly attractive, it would feel like a life sentence.

She was in an unenviable situation and wasn't sure that she could cope. It wasn't simply the fear of their impending marriage. There were other issues. Had anyone given any thought to her business? Who was going to look after that in her absence? Why would everyone think she could give it up just like that?

Except that she had a very capable assistant. Kate could run the business single-handed. She was making excuses here. There was no solid reason why she couldn't marry Vidal.

Elena flew back to LA the next day, shocking Kate with the news that she was going to get married.

'Can you look after the business for a while?' she asked, not daring to tell her assistant yet that it would be for a whole year.

'Can I?' Kate's face was radiant. 'Take as much time off as you like. You know everything will be in safe hands. Oh, I'm going to love this. You're sure you trust me?'

'Completely.'

'Was it love at first sight? Oh, my God, it's so romantic. Did you ever envisage planning your own wedding?'

Elena shook her head. 'I was never going to get married. Believe me, it's as much a shock to me as it is to you.'

The shock lasted until she returned to Spain and Vidal turned up at the house saying he had come to take her out to dinner. Her heart went into overdrive. Her mother, out of hospital by this time, was flustered, her father grateful, but Elena couldn't even look at him. This was the man she was going to marry, this was the man she was going to live and sleep with for the next year. Was it any wonder her heart felt as though it were trying to escape from her ribcage?

Vidal himself showed no sign of hysteria. In fact, his composure was admirable. 'You'll excuse me if I take Elena away from you,' he said to her parents. 'We have a wedding to plan.'

Elena hated the nonchalant way he said it. *A wedding to plan.* He made it sound as ordinary as if he had said they were going out to dinner. Except that her mother's eyes shone. 'Of course, Vidal. Of course. And thank you. Thank you very much.'

Once in his limousine, sharing the back seat, there was no escape.

'Look at me, Elena.'

Up until that point she had rigidly refused to meet his

eyes. It was enough feeling his presence, feeling a sense of shock that the attraction she'd tried to tell herself she had imagined was still there, still very real. She had thought about him constantly all the time she'd been in LA. The image of the strong lines of his face, those dangerously attractive eyes, would not go away. They had penetrated her dreams as well as her daytime thoughts.

Reluctantly she turned her head and instantly wished that she hadn't when she met the silver intensity of his gaze. And once their eyes met she couldn't look away. There was something in their depths that electrified her soul. He did not even have to speak to make her feel like this. Simply looking at him, feeling the magnetic power in those amazing eyes, stealing a glance at his beautifully moulded mouth, wondering what it would be like to feel those lips against hers in a deeply passionate kiss—not the sort he had given her earlier—was enough to warn her that she needed to be careful.

Very careful.

These were dangerous feelings. This marriage wasn't going to be for real. She mustn't let herself get carried away and lose all sense of direction. It was for one year. Twelve months. Three hundred and sixty five days. That was all.

If she wasn't sitting right next to him and her mind was working properly she could have divided it into hours and minutes, seconds even. And afterwards it would end. She and Vidal would go their different ways. The job would be done.

The job! How had she got herself into this? How was she going to go through with it?

'What are you thinking?'

'That I must be crazy,' she answered without thinking.

'If you're crazy then I've never seen a more beautiful crazy woman.' During the few days that he'd been away Vidal hadn't been able to get Elena out of his mind. She had danced before his eyes night and day. The meetings he'd attended had held his attention for a few hours at a time, but once they were over the amazing Elena had been back in his thoughts.

He couldn't wait to make her his bride and take her to bed. He actually wanted to make love to her this very minute, but he knew that if he took things too quickly she might very well back out of the whole thing.

She smelled gorgeous. He didn't know what the perfume was called, probably Aphrodisiac. If it wasn't it should be. He hadn't felt like this since—since when? The truth was he had never felt like this in his whole life.

Elena had an inner beauty, an untouched air about her, and he desperately wanted to find out what made her tick. It was the biggest wonder in the world that some other guy hadn't snapped her up. Would she be hot in bed? Experienced? Or a total novice? His groin ached at the very thought. So many questions, so much he needed to discover about her. But where to begin? How to make her feel at ease?

At this moment she looked as though she wanted to be anywhere but here. Her incredible eyes were shaded by long silky lashes, her full and tempting lips pressed tightly together. He was not used to women backing away from him.

'Are you scared of me, Elena?' It wasn't what he'd

wanted to say, but the words had slipped out before he could stop them.

With a toss of her head her thick black fringe fell over one eye, making her look coquettish, though he knew that that was the last thing she would want. Coquettishness was not Elena's style.

'Is that what you think? Actually, I was wondering why we need to talk. Our families can arrange the wedding. There's nothing that you and I need to do. Just turn up,' she added bitterly.

'Not so, Elena.' He felt a flash of anger at her apparent indifference. 'You need to choose your wedding dress, your bridesmaids, and we should shop together for rings. Then there's the guest list—we should have a say in that. There's a whole host of stuff to do. I'll happily leave some of the organising to our parents, but there's still plenty for us if we're to make this marriage look genuine.'

'But it isn't genuine,' she retorted with another flash of her spectacular eyes.

'No one is going to know that,' he cautioned, his silver eyes growing fierce. 'No one. Do you understand?'

Elena nodded. Nevertheless her eyes warred with his. 'I should tell you now that I'm not a good actress.'

'You won't need to be,' he growled, and forgetting the warning he had given himself earlier, he hooked a hand lightly behind her neck and lowered his head to hers.

Elena had known what would happen when he kissed her again. It was why she had kept her distance, why she had not let him see by the merest movement of her eyes that she was turned on by him. And now it was too late.

The instant his mouth touched hers she went up in flames. Without conscious thought her lips parted and the feelings that raced through her were volcanic. It was as though her whole body had erupted. As though it had been waiting for this moment all its life and was going to take full advantage.

When Vidal felt her response he groaned and deepened the kiss, instantly setting off a further chain reaction until her whole body felt reborn, newly sensitised, dangerously explosive.

One tiny part of her couldn't believe that this was happening and warned her to back away now. On the rare occasions she had thought about marriage she had had the ideal man in her head. She wanted someone with the same ambition as herself, someone prepared to launch out in a new direction and take chances. She had worked hard and surpassed her wildest dreams.

Vidal had worked hard too, very hard, extremely hard in fact, but he had remained in the banking industry, following his father's footsteps, and that in anyone's eyes would have made him boring.

And yet boring was most certainly not a word she associated with Vidal. How could a man who looked as good as he did be uninteresting? How could a man who twisted her nerves to screaming point be dull? Or who kissed her with dangerous gentleness? He was the devil incarnate. A man sent to test her, to bend her to his will without her even realising it.

His kiss was not just a kiss. It was a kiss to surpass all kisses. His mouth was not hot and hard, it wasn't demanding even. But it was all the more treacherous because of its gentleness.

It was she who wanted more, who wanted to feel the fire in him, the urgency, the evidence that he truly desired her. Because how could they go through with this marriage if he didn't?

As if her wishes had somehow transferred themselves to him, Vidal's long, strong fingers moulded the back of her head, urging them closer and harder together. His kisses became more demanding, his tongue exploring her mouth, tangling with her tongue, encouraging her to do the same to him.

With her whole body now on fire Elena knew that if they had been anywhere but here she would have begged him to make love to her. She couldn't have helped herself. He had awoken the animal inside her. Indeed she might not have had to beg because one glance at his face and she saw her own torment echoed there.

It was not until the car slowed to a halt that they pulled away from each other and Elena couldn't help wondering how they were going to sit at their dinner table and pretend that they didn't want to be in bed.

She was almost afraid to look Vidal in the eye, but he had no such compunction. 'I think,' he said softly, a meaningful smile curving his lips, 'that I'm going to enjoy being married to you, Elena Valero.'

CHAPTER FOUR

Vidal knew that bedding Elena before their marriage was out of bounds—no matter how much he wanted her, and that was one hell of a lot. His body was tortured with need and ached so much that he felt he would go out of his mind.

After that kiss—the all-important, ground-breaking, manic kiss in the back of his car, when he had felt a whole host of raw emotions, when she had returned it with a fiery hunger of her own—Elena had frozen on him, making it very clear that she did not want a repeat performance.

Whether she had scared herself by her instant re-action he did not know, but he certainly had no inten-tion of keeping her at arm's length after their wedding. *Dios!* He wasn't made of ice. How could a man keep his hands off such a woman who besides torturing him with her sizzling, supple body could kiss so hotly and willingly?

It had been the most surprising, the most amazing kiss. One he had never expected, but which had given so much of herself away. Elena was certainly a hot-blooded woman with the potential to carry them both into a world where nothing mattered except erotic sensations and mind-blowing sex. He had the feeling that with Elena he would experience something new every day, something incredible and exciting, and his tortured mind was already spinning away to a planet of its own.

They had spent the evening talking about their wedding and he had spent the night dreaming about her deliciously tempting body next to his, making electrical, uncontrolled, unstoppable love, and he consoled himself with the fact that he would have a whole year of this undeniably stimulating pleasure before he finally got her out of his system.

Which he had no doubt he would. He fancied her like hell, but marriage—long term? It would never work. From what little he had gleaned from her sister she had moved to America to have a good time. She'd felt no commitment to family. Which in his eyes meant that she wouldn't make a good wife or mother. Which was just as well because he wasn't ready to settle down yet.

A lover, yes, an instantly excitable lover, but no more. And he had twelve months of spectacular lovemaking to look forward to. Elena in his bed every night, himself inside her. She had the potential to be like no other lover he'd ever had. Everything in him cried out for fulfilment.

And one way or another he intended on taking it.

Elena was not happy when the next day Vidal insisted that they go shopping for their wedding rings. Dinner had been an uncomfortable affair. She ought never to have allowed Vidal's kiss to affect her, she shouldn't even have let him kiss her, and she still couldn't understand why she had reacted as she did. And she was even more alarmed when he took her to Seville's most exclusive jeweller and they were ushered into a private back room.

The owner, a friend of Vidal's, brought out exquisite diamond after exquisite diamond, each one more beautiful than the last. But Elena didn't want to choose. It didn't feel right. Why should he spend so much money when their marriage was a sham?

But as usual Vidal got his own way. He personally placed each ring on her finger, doing so with such tenderness that Elena wanted to scream. Was he aware of the torture he was putting her through? Did he know that his touch, the same as his kisses, sent a dangerous, convoluted agony through her? He was deliberately behaving like the most attentive lover of all time.

In the end she walked out of the shop wearing the biggest solitaire diamond she had ever seen. Their wedding rings, also chosen, were being kept in the shop's vault until their wedding day.

'It was wrong of you to inflict this ring on me,' she scolded in the car on their way home, twisting it round and round on her finger. It felt heavy and alien and she was so afraid that she might lose it.

'You don't like it? We can always—'

'It's not a case of liking it,' she protested angrily. 'It makes far too much of a statement.'

'You think I'm not proud to be marrying you?'

'Of course you're not,' she snapped. 'Pride doesn't enter into it. Let's face it, neither of us want this wedding. We're saving the bank, that's all.'

'And you think your parents' bank isn't worth a diamond ring?'

'It's not just any diamond,' she retorted. 'It was the most expensive in the shop. It doesn't impress me, though I suppose you think it will impress other people. Tell them how much you love me. If only they knew.' She was glad of the glass window between them and his driver because she would have hated him to hear this conversation.

'You're not playing the game, Elena.' Vidal's voice was quiet but deadly.

'That's because I'm not into playing games,' she declared with a flash of her beautiful eyes.

'Mmm,' he growled. 'Perhaps you've never played the right sort. Perhaps you have a lot to learn.'

He looked as though he wanted to kiss her!

She certainly had a lot to learn about defending herself where Vidal was concerned. He was dangerous. He infiltrated her senses, he turned everything on inside her, he made her wish that she were anywhere but in his presence because there was no chance of ignoring him.

'I think we should hire a wedding planner to organise the wedding,' he said with a complete and surprising change of subject. 'I don't want to take any risks. I want everything to be perfect.'

Elena shook her head dismissively. 'Don't waste your money. I'll do it. It will give me something to do, otherwise goodness knows how I'll occupy my time.'

'It's going to be a big wedding.' Vidal's eyes were sceptical as he looked at Elena. 'I doubt you'd be up to it.'

'Not up to it?' she snapped, her eyes flashing hotly, hating his very low opinion of her. 'It's what I do for a living.' If he'd taken an interest instead of using her as a free ride towards his dream of acquiring their bank then he would have known.

'You're a wedding planner?' he enquired, a frown now dragging his brows together, looking at her closely as if seeing her for the first time.

'That's right.'

'You work for a wedding-planning company?' Stupid question, of course she must, hadn't she just told him? Heavens, why had he never bothered to ask what she'd been doing in America? Why had he made a fool of himself by only just finding out? What was wrong with him?

He guessed it was because their marriage was a means to an end. There was no love or romance involved. It was a business proposition. A twelve-month contract. In normal, everyday business dealings he didn't know all the personal details of everyone he dealt with. Wasn't it the same thing?

Somewhere inside him he began to feel uncomfortable. And he didn't like it, not one little bit.

Elena tilted her chin, her eyes steady on his. 'I own the company.'

And now he felt worse. If she had said that she was a man dressed as a woman she couldn't have shocked him more. His mind reeled. 'And you've left your business in order to help out your parents?'

'That's about the sum of it,' she answered coolly. 'But of course none of that bothered you, did it?'

He chose to ignore her question. 'I take it that you don't have a very big order book?' If she could afford to take a year off it didn't say very much for her company.

'And what's that supposed to mean?' she snapped.

'That I'm not doing very well? On the contrary.' Her eyes flashed defensively. 'I'm doing *very well* for myself, thank you.'

'I see.'

That was all he said. She must have stunned him by her admission. For the first time since agreeing to marry him Elena felt good inside. 'And fortuitously I happen to have a very capable assistant who is looking after things for me while I'm—away. Things might have been very different if I didn't have Kate to depend on. I know you think that all I am interested in is a good time, but on the contrary, Vidal, I work very hard. And I'm not happy about having to walk away from it for twelve whole months.'

'So tell me about LA,' he said, his silver eyes level on hers. 'It's not somewhere I've ever visited.'

'Then you should,' she retorted. 'It's a vibrant, cosmopolitan city and actually Spanish is well spoken there. You can shop till you drop, there's a fabulous nightlife, and the people are extremely friendly. My clientele includes film stars and business people such as yourself.'

'So you shop on Rodeo Drive, is that it? You mix with the rich and famous. I'm impressed.'

The words were easily spoken, but he didn't look impressed. In fact, he looked anything but and Elena wished that she were anywhere but here in this car with him having this conversation.

'I never realised that you were such a high flier. No one told me, not even your sister.'

'That's because you've shown not the least bit of interest in what I do—what I did,' she corrected quickly.

'I don't even believe that you feel sorry for my parents, I still think your main aim is to get your hands on their bank.'

In the long silence that followed Vidal shot her a look that almost sliced the floor from beneath her feet. 'If that's your opinion then let's forget the whole deal. I can assure you, Elena, that I'm not doing this for any selfish reasons. We don't have to go through with it. The choice is yours. Feel free to let your parents down if that's what you want to do.'

The air in the car had thickened and Elena wished that she had held her tongue. It wouldn't be herself or Vidal who suffered if she backed out now; it would be her parents. Especially her mother. Could she do this to them? Of course not. But it took every ounce of pride to admit that she was in the wrong.

'I'm sorry, I shouldn't have said that. Of course we must go through with it.'

Vidal nodded, his eyes studying hers for several long seconds until finally his shoulders relaxed. 'I am not a greedy person, Elena, despite what you might think. I am a businessman and the merger makes sound business sense. And now that I've discovered you have a good business brain on that pretty head of yours, I have a suggestion to make.'

Elena widened her eyes suspiciously. Any suggestions from Vidal could only spell more trouble.

'How do you feel about coming to work for me after the wedding? Purely for the duration of our marriage, of course. You'll naturally want to get back to your own business as soon as the twelve months is up, but it will give you something to do in the meantime. I'm impressed with your organisational skills. I could do with someone like you. And you'll be keeping an eye on your own business, of course?'

'If I'm given the time,' she retorted, her eyes meeting his head-on. How she managed not to look away she had no idea, but somehow she did it. She was well aware that she had given Vidal a shock and his offer of a job was as a result of it. Up till then he hadn't had a very good opinion of her.

Vidal's eyes narrowed dangerously. 'How about my offer?'

'I'll let you know.' He had shocked her by suggesting she work with him, but there were too many other things on her mind at this moment to give it any real thought. It could be a good thing, as he said it would give her something to do; on the other hand it could be sheer hell. It would mean she would never escape him.

During the next few days and weeks Vidal couldn't help but be impressed with the amount of work Elena put in. No one would have guessed that their marriage wasn't for real. She really was pulling out all the stops.

'You're doing an amazing job,' he told her one evening when he had again taken her out to dinner. 'Anyone would think this was a real marriage with the attention you're paying to detail. No one will ever guess that it's all make-believe, that this isn't your lifelong dream. Thank you, Elena.'

Elena didn't need thanks. In fact, she was hardly listening. It was bizarre to think that she had been planning her own wedding—to a man she did not love and to whom she had no intention of staying married!

And it had been even harder fending off the paparazzi. How they knew about the wedding she didn't know, but they were followed wherever they went, their photographs appeared in all the newspapers, the story of Vidal turning from one sister to another was discussed and explored and laid bare for everyone to read.

It was hell.

Vidal's younger brother, Fernan, who knew about the deal and had arrived for the wedding, thought the whole thing was farcical. 'I think my brother needs his head examined,' he said to Elena. 'If I were marrying you I'd want it to be for ever.'

'He's a gentleman and he's helping my family.' Elena lifted her chin and fastened cold eyes on his face. Fernan was equally as good-looking as Vidal, equally tall, and looked after the overseas interests of the bank. He had been a good companion to her when they were younger, but there had been no contact between them over the years.

'And no doubt helping himself to an affair with you in the bargain?' came the cynical reply. 'I don't blame Reina for running out on him—it's a huge commitment. Be careful, Elena. Do not fall in love with him or you'll have your heart broken.'

'You need have no fear,' she tossed back, her eyes flashing. 'I'm giving him twelve months of my life and not a minute more. It's the least I can do under the circumstances.'

'Okay. But remember that if you should ever need a shoulder to cry on, I'm here.'

On the eve of their wedding Vidal turned up at Elena's house and placed a package into her hand.

'What is this?' she asked, recognising the wrapping from the same jeweller where he had purchased their rings.

'A present for you, *mi amor.*'

Elena frowned. 'But why?'

'Because it needed to be done,' he exclaimed impatiently. 'What would people think if I didn't shower you with gifts? Open it.'

But Elena's fingers were impossibly clumsy and in the end he pulled the wrapping off for her. The white satin box, fastened with gold cord, revealed an awesomely expensive diamond necklace. From the fine chain hung a pendant in the shape of two entwined circles each studded with flawless diamonds. And sitting beside it was a pair of matching earrings.

'I can't accept this,' she said breathlessly. 'Even though they are the most beautiful things I have ever seen.'

'But you must,' insisted Vidal. 'A beautiful gift for a beautiful lady. The necklace will look sensational on your skin. Allow me to put it on so that you can see for yourself.'

He positioned her in front of a mirror and Elena could see the concentration on his face as he fastened it around her throat. His fingers burned where they touched her skin, creating a whole host of unwanted emotions. It took all of her will power not to turn in his arms and kiss him. He looked so handsome, so utterly gorgeous, so incredibly sexy, that it was torture resisting him. Her whole body ached with a need so deep that it hurt.

'There, don't you agree?' he asked gruffly when he

had finished and stepped back so that she could study herself.

'It's perfect,' she said huskily. 'But you shouldn't have spent so much money when—'

He silenced her with the touch of his lips to hers. Not a lover's kiss, but the sort one would give a child, or a parent. Nevertheless it sent a million tiny shivers down her spine, and a further host of explosive sensations through every one of her veins.

She shivered. 'Thank you, Vidal.' Her tone was so soft that she wasn't sure he had heard—until he smiled and nodded.

'The pleasure is all mine.'

That night Elena lay in bed with her eyes closed, but she was as far away from falling asleep as she was from the moon. All she could see in front of her mind's eye was Vidal. Tall, handsome, charismatic, a devastatingly magnetic man. A man who could melt her with one glance.

But a man she did not love!

The only spark between them was a sexual one. And that had been suppressed since their first condemning kiss. Painfully so on her part at times. But since she was the one who had declared they must wait...

Without a doubt Vidal would insist on her sharing his bed tomorrow night. He had made that very clear. In fact, she was surprised that he had held off for so long. She had thought he would ignore her request, persuade her to think differently, and indeed there had been occasions when she had willed him to do so.

But no, Vidal had remained true to his word.

There were over two hundred guests expected, show-business stars, business acquaintances, family he hadn't seen in years. Some had already arrived and she'd been showered with congratulations and questions. It had been particularly difficult fending off queries as to where her sister was, but somehow she had got through the day.

All she had to do now was get through tomorrow.

Her wedding dress was a dream in layers of organza and silk. Her mother helped her and the bridesmaids get ready and she had tears in her eyes the whole time. Elena's make-up had been professionally done, her hair too, but now it was just herself and her mother, her bridesmaids having skipped away to show off their dresses to anyone who cared to look.

'You look beautiful, Elena,' her parent said softly. 'No one would ever guess that you're not totally in love. Or have you fallen for Vidal? Some days I wonder.'

'Oh, *Mamá*, of course I don't love him,' she answered promptly. 'But it's such a beautiful dress, and he gave me such magnificent jewellery—' she touched the incredible necklace '—how can I not get carried away?'

'I thought you'd be terrified. It's a big thing that you're doing. We really do appreciate it.'

Elena hugged her mother. 'I know, and if it makes you happy then it's worth it.'

Her three little bridesmaids—cousins of Vidal— wore deep pink fairy-tale dresses that matched the roses in the church and in her bridal bouquet. Everything had been co-ordinated right down to the last petal and Elena was rightly proud of what she had achieved.

A celebrity magazine was covering the event for their

thousands of readers, generating even more interest; television cameramen were there as well, and as Elena made her way into the church on her father's arm she felt incredibly nervous. It seemed as if the whole world were watching.

If they had any idea that it was all a sham she would die on the spot. She had to be strong and brave now and act as she had never acted before.

Vidal looked devilishly handsome in his dark suit and he took her hand as she joined him at the altar. 'You look stunning, Elena. I'm very proud of you.'

His assurance helped, but it was not easy—she was trembling all over, especially when the time came to repeat her wedding vows. She could hear the nerves in her voice and was sure everyone else could too. How could she do this knowing that there was no love involved?

She had always dreamed of her wedding day. Of the love that would radiate out from her and her husband-to-be. It would be the best day of her life, one that she would remember for ever.

So how could she go through with this loveless marriage?

She couldn't!

Everyone was waiting for her to continue. To vow unswerving love for the rest of her life.

She couldn't do it!

She turned, taking a tiny step away from Vidal, and heard the communal gasp from the congregation.

Then, standing out clearly from the rest of the congregation, she saw her mother's pale and anxious face, her father with his arm about her shoulders, supporting her, and immediately Elena knew that she had to carry on regardless of what the future held. It wasn't just that she was saving the bank, her mother's life depended on it as well, and she loved her mother dearly. There was no way in this world that she could let her down.

Vidal touched her arm and Elena turned back to him, her face pale but composed.

Her wedding ring lay heavy on her finger and she felt uncomfortable as she finally finished repeating her vows, as they were pronounced man and wife, when Vidal kissed her.

'You can tell me later what happened,' he muttered as they both dutifully smiled while the photographs were being taken, adding swiftly, 'It's a stunning dress—did I tell you that? But I can't wait to strip it off you and take you to bed.'

Elena felt hot colour flood her cheeks. In truth, despite the fact that she had almost cut and run, it was what she hungered for too, but to hear Vidal say it made it sound wrong. 'You shouldn't be talking like this, especially not in front of our guests. Don't forget, Vidal, that this isn't a real marriage.'

For just a second fierce darkness filled his eyes and his grip on her arms tightened. Then his face relaxed and he smiled, but his voice, low enough for no one to hear except herself, was like steel. 'I don't want to hear you speak like that again, Elena.' He moved his mouth closer to her ear. 'No more talk of our marriage not being real. Smile—it is what our guests expect.'

The reception was held in the banqueting hall of one of Seville's finest hotels and when Elena felt that she could take no more, when she could smile no more, when the pressure of the day had built up to such an extent that once again she felt like screaming and running, she excused herself and hurried away to the sanctity of the ladies' room.

It was empty and for a few peaceful minutes she was able to shut out everything that was going on around her. She ran cold water over her wrists and tried to pretend that the last few hours had never happened—except that she had an enormously expensive wedding ring on her finger. There was no denying the fact that she was stuck with Vidal for the next year whether she liked it or not.

It took every ounce of determination not to run away—as far as she could, as quickly as she could. Tears trickled down her cheeks. Why, oh, why, was this happening to her?

Out there she now had a husband whom she did not love. Someone whose bed she would have to share. Her face flamed at the thought. Because in all honesty that part of it would not be such a hard deal.

Vidal had the power to turn her on simply by looking at her. Whether it was something he had perfected over the years to get his women she did not know. And it mattered not. The truth was those silver eyes were dangerously seductive. She had only to look into them to feel her defences melting.

Which, she supposed, was a good thing, because marriage to a man whom she did not feel remotely attracted to would have been sheer hell. At least they had something going in their favour.

Elena repaired her make-up, assured herself that she looked normal—or at least as normal as someone who had just got married for convenience could look—and made her way back out.

Vidal must have been watching for her because he instantly appeared at her side, a faint frown creasing his brow. 'You've been a long time. I was going to send someone in after you.'

It was said in good humour, but Elena heard an undertone of criticism. 'Isn't a lady allowed a few minutes to herself?' she asked sharply. 'You have no idea what I've gone through today.'

'Tell me,' he suggested softly. 'Does it have anything to do with the fact that you almost ran away at the church?'

Elena closed her eyes briefly, letting out her breath on long, silent sigh. 'How could I expect you to understand the enormity of it all? You're right, I did want to run away, but—'

She was totally unprepared for what happened next. Vidal dragged her up on to the stage where the band was playing and took over the microphone.

'I know I've already thanked everyone for coming and making this day very special for my wife and I.' He smiled at Elena, his eyes more tender than she had ever seen them. And he took her hand into his, squeezing it reassuringly.

Elena wanted to cringe and run, but he was making very sure that she didn't.

'But now I'd like to take a few more moments of your time by saying how very proud I am of Elena. For those of you who don't know, she is a professional wedding planner and I think you will agree that today's events could not be surpassed.'

Loud clapping and cheering followed and Elena felt herself blush from his praise.

'I hadn't seen Elena for many years,' he continued. 'And it was fate when she and I met again. It was meant to be. And it will be.'

The whole room filled with applause. Vidal felt Elena trembling at his side and without conscious thought he pulled her against him and kissed her. It was the only thing he could think of to reassure her. It resulted in more cheers and more clapping.

He felt her heart throbbing wildly against him, like a bird trapped in a cage.

'Never mind, *mi amor*, it will soon be over,' he murmured softly against her mouth. 'You've done your parents proud today.'

And tonight, in his bed, she would hopefully do him proud. It had been agony keeping his hands off her these last few weeks. It had stretched his limits. On more than one occasion he had felt that he would crack, that he wouldn't be able to keep his promise.

But finally the day was here when he could claim her body, when he could release the demons that had been driving him crazy. He had no intention of forcing himself on her. He was prepared to be patient, take things slowly, confident that Elena would melt in his arms before the night was out.

He recalled the way she had responded to his kisses that day in the car, and his whole body ignited at the thought of her in his bed tonight. There was to be no honeymoon, he had told everyone they were postponing it because of business commitments. Instead they were spending their first night here in the hotel honeymoon suite, and then moving tomorrow to his house on the outskirts of the city.

By the time their last guests had gone Elena had worked herself up into such a state that Vidal was worried. 'Are you not feeling well? You look very pale. Has it all been too much for you?'

'What do you think?' Elena asked fiercely, feeling no need now to put on a front. 'I can't believe I've been foolish enough to let myself get sucked into such a charade.' Or was it the fact that tonight she would be sharing Vidal's bed? Was this what was shredding her nerves?

She was pleased that she had helped her parents out, that went without saying, but at what cost? Until this moment she hadn't properly realised the enormity of what she was doing. Marrying Vidal she could face. But sleeping with him? Pretending to the whole world that theirs was a normal marriage was way too much.

By the time they eventually took the lift up to their suite Elena had made up her mind that she was not going to let him make love to her. No way! Not under any circumstances! It was too big an ask. He'd have to make do with her sharing his home, but not his bed.

Until the bedroom door closed behind them!

CHAPTER FIVE

EVERY promise Elena had made to herself was forgotten. She was aware of nothing except Vidal's hard, virile body against hers. The feel of him, the shape of him, the way his thighs touched hers sending tremors all the way down to her toes. The way his hips ground into her, the beat of his heart against her breasts. It was a solid thud compared to her own frantic rush of emotion.

Then there was the scent of him, the faint lingering odour of the cologne he'd splashed on earlier in the day, the clean smell of his breath, the drugging male scent of his arousal.

She pulled herself up short at that thought. Vidal was all male, that was for sure. And he had an indefinable something that made her aware of his hunger for her.

Elena's fingers sought and found the solid strength in his shoulders as his head bowed down to hers. He had already flung off his jacket and the fine cotton of his shirt hid none of the power packed into those muscles. She felt them flex as his arms tightened around her, as he imprisoned her in a circle from which there was no escape. And at this moment she did not want to be free. Every thought of denying herself the pleasure had gone.

One touch was all it had taken to make her insanely aware of Vidal and all he could give her. From the moment they had been pronounced man and wife he had hardly left her side. They had laughed together and pretended together. Both sets of parents had stood proudly and watched and no one, but no one, had guessed that it wasn't a love match.

So did the throbbing of her heart tell her that she was already beginning to feel something more for Vidal? Or was it simply a case of raw sexual hunger? Something she had felt when they first met to discuss this bizarre situation. An instant flare of desire. It was alien and yet at the same time it felt so right. Even her body told her that it craved fulfilment.

With the feel of Vidal's lips on hers, and the treacherous hunger building up in her lower belly, Elena dared to look into his face. She had instinctively closed her eyes when his mouth claimed hers, allowing herself to forget everything except what he was doing, but now her lids flickered open—and shocked themselves wide when they met his steady silver ones!

They were narrowed and intent and filled with something she couldn't read, and she wondered how long he had been watching her. Had she laid bare all her feelings? Was that why he had made a move on her so quickly and so surely? Because he had been aware that she was having second thoughts?

'You taste good enough to eat,' he murmured against her mouth, his voice gruffer and deeper than she had ever heard it. Full of animal hunger.

'Mmm,' was all she could manage in response. She could taste brandy on his lips, but it reminded her of how little he had actually drunk. Clearly he had wanted to keep himself alert for this very moment. He had known she wouldn't want a drunken husband forcing himself on her.

His kiss deepened, his tongue exploring inside her mouth now, an agony of fear and delight whistling through her mind. Her head fell back in silent submission, her tongue dancing with his, faint groans escaping the back of her throat. She was giving too much of herself away, but she couldn't help it.

Ever since she'd come back home and discovered this new excitingly sexy Vidal she had known that it was inevitable. It wasn't a case of being in love with him. He was simply a man whose sexuality could not be ignored. She'd like to bet that each woman he encountered felt the same. There was something about him that awoke every female hormone in her body.

It was a unique blend of hunger and fear and she did not wish to deny it. Not any longer. She had spent the last weeks trying to ignore the feelings that chased through her body every time they were together. Now she could contain them no longer.

When his lips moved from her mouth to make an excruciatingly slow descent down the arch of her throat she heard herself cry out his name, 'Vidal…' And her legs suddenly felt as though they were no longer capable of holding her up.

'Vidal, what?'

She heard the smile in his voice as he slid one arm down to the small of her back so that she was bent slightly over it, while his other caressed the side of her face, touching her lips where his mouth had been, tracing her high cheekbones, the delicate lobes of her ears, and all the time his mouth moved ever lower.

Elena felt her blood screaming through her veins, felt as though all her birthdays had come together. It was a whole and totally new experience. She'd had boyfriends in the past, yes, but none who had created this same storm inside her. She feared meltdown—and he hadn't yet started!

Earlier she had changed out of her wedding finery into a strapless emerald-green dress and without her knowing it Vidal's knowing fingers had inched down the zip. The dress had built-in support, so when her naked breasts were suddenly exposed to his greedy eyes she gasped out loud.

He growled something deep and unintelligible as his mouth began a fresh assault. At the same time her hips were ground against his and she could feel the full impact of his awakening. It was both scary and exciting at the same time.

Vidal felt like shouting for help. Each time Elena moved she rubbed against the part of him that throbbed with need, increasing his hunger a hundredfold. He ached and burned with such fierce longing that he found it hard to keep control.

Yet he knew that he must. He knew that if he took things too quickly he could easily scare her away. It had been hard enough these last few weeks; he had thought they would last for ever. And he wanted now to enjoy the delights of her body, but he wanted Elena to enjoy it too.

When she once again wriggled explosively against him he couldn't contain a groan from deep in his throat and without another thought he slid both arms beneath her and lifted her onto the bed. Her dress fell readily to the floor, leaving her wearing nothing but a dainty white thong. Her sensationally long bronzed limbs and her gently rounded breasts with their high nipples tempted him beyond reason.

In a matter of seconds he discarded his own clothes, but it was not until he lay down beside her that he realised how fast his breathing had become.

Her eyes had never left him. They shone like stars, hugely expressive, telling him that she wanted this as much as he did. He couldn't believe his fortune that Elena had turned into such a stunning, beautiful, sexy young woman.

He wanted to make love to her all night through.

And the best thing about it, Elena was ready for him too.

Never in her whole life had Elena wanted a man as much as she wanted Vidal now. It was as though the feelings she had suppressed during the last weeks had built into one big crescendo of hunger and need. She was ready for Vidal to make wonderful, magical, intensely exciting love. She was prepared to be swept along on a tide of passion. Let Vidal tease her into making heart-racing, blood-pounding, mind-blowing sex.

Her thong was discarded with the flick of a wrist, his knowing fingers torturing and teasing the secret heart of her until she felt that she was going out of her mind. When she could stand no more, when she felt that Vidal too was reaching a point of no return, he lowered himself over her.

'This is all right for you?' he asked huskily.

Was it all right? What a stupid question. She wouldn't be here if it wasn't.

And yet, even though she was under the impression that she wanted Vidal to make love to her more than anything else, the moment he tried to enter her she froze. It was an entirely involuntary reaction and she couldn't believe that it was happening, and yet it was and there was nothing she could do about it.

Her body was telling her that this was not the right thing to do. That having intercourse when she had married this man for reasons other than love was wrong. And yet how could it be when her hormones had been on high alert? When she had even assured Vidal that it was what she desired?

She had let herself get carried away; her head had ruled her heart. But her heart had known best. If it hadn't sent out warning signals, stopping her from taking that last step, she would have become Vidal's in every way possible. It would have been the beginning of twelve months of perfect lovemaking.

Vidal had everything. Looks, sex appeal, charm, magnetism, dynamism. You name it, he had it. Add to that a keen brain and a ferociously active mind, he was not a man who could be ignored under any circumstances. So why was her body denying herself him?

She would like to bet that everyone at the bank stood to attention when he entered the room. And his female conquests? They would fall at his feet too. Just as she had done. And even though some totally unexpected part of her brain had suddenly held her back she somehow knew that it would be impossible to keep him at arm's length for ever.

'Elena, what is wrong?' he asked concernedly, pulling back at once. 'Did I hurt you?'

'No, of course you didn't. I—I don't know. Vidal. I'm sorry. I couldn't help myself.'

She was sorry for both Vidal and herself. Strangely her body still hungered to feel him inside her, to be so close that they became one, to feel his strength and his power, and to overflow with joy when they finally reached their climax.

But it was not to be. Not tonight anyway. She felt tears trickle down her cheeks and was startled when Vidal swept them away with a gentle finger. 'Perhaps I was asking too much, too soon. It has been a big day for you. I will wait—until you are ready, *querida*. We should try to get some sleep.'

Elena couldn't believe he was being so understanding. He had been almost at the point of no return. What must he have thought? Why wasn't he angry? Not that she wanted him to be, but his understanding puzzled her and in fact made her feel even worse.

She lay carefully on the edge of the bed, so far away from him that she was in danger of falling off. The trouble was she was so aware of him that it was sheer hell lying there stiff and silent—and naked! And she felt incredibly guilty for what she had done.

She could come up with no plausible explanation for the way her body had reacted. It didn't make sense because, even now, just thinking about him lying only inches away from her sent a flurry of sensation through her most intimate parts. Dare she ask him to try again? Or would it be another disaster? She curled up into the foetal position, afraid now, afraid that it might happen every time. Afraid that he might lose patience with her and tell her that the deal was off.

And what would her parents do then? How would the news affect her mother? It didn't bear thinking about.

At least Vidal was being understanding—for now! But how long would it last?

She jumped out of bed, unable to lie there any longer, pulled on the cream silk negligee that she had bought especially for tonight, and walked round to his side of the bed.

'I really am sorry, Vidal, for letting you down.'

'Elena, you don't need to keep apologising.' He sat up, his legs over the edge, totally unconcerned by his nakedness.

Elena knew that she must keep her eyes on his face, but it was difficult when his magnificent bronzed chest with its fine covering of silky, dark hairs simply begged to be touched.

It wasn't only his chest that was bare, but every part of him. Only once did her eyes drop lower. She couldn't stop them. It was a quick glance and back again but it set off a fresh burning desire between her legs and she had to ask herself the question. What had stopped her earlier?

Amazingly Vidal was still ready for her. It was what he wanted, what she wanted too—*in her mind*!

'I'll try not to let it happen again,' she said softly.

Vidal closed his eyes. Just what had happened here he wasn't sure. One moment Elena had been eager to make love, she had felt amazing in his arms, her body soft and willing, her perfume teasing his nostrils. Everything about the moment had been right. And then suddenly she had closed down.

Was it simply that she had been trying too hard to please him, then when it came to the point of no return she couldn't go through with it? Was what he was asking of her too enormous?

He cringed inside. *Infierno*, what sort of a man was he? He had never forced a woman into anything against her will. It went against every instinct. So why had he felt compelled to take Elena now? Was he crazy or what? Was he going out of his mind—seduced by a pretty face and a lithesome body? What was happening to him? Didn't he have any ethics left?

'Do not apologise, Elena,' he said gruffly, looking up into her troubled face. 'It was my fault. In my arrogance I demanded that you share my bed and my body. I should have given you time to adjust. It was tactless of me.'

Elena's pretty eyes widened, her eyelids fluttering delicately, two spots of high colour in her cheeks. 'I— I didn't think you'd take it like this. I thought—'

Vidal put a firm finger over her lips. 'Time is not of the essence. I can be patient.' He was actually feeling something akin to guilt here. And he was not used to feeling guilty. He didn't like the feeling. Nevertheless he was aware that he had caused Elena some distress and this didn't sit well on his shoulders.

If only she weren't so excitingly sexy. She had looked fantastic today and his body hungered and ached for her, so much so that it was like a physical pain. She still looked stunning even without make-up, even with the trace of tears down her face, even without all her wedding finery. Her dress had been a sensation, but he preferred her without it.

What he really wanted to do was snatch off her negligee and kiss away her tears and play beautiful games with her for the rest of the night. He wanted to tease and arouse her so completely that her body wouldn't back down again. He wanted her moulded to him, he wanted to be beside her and inside her. Even thinking about it caused an erection that he knew Elena could see.

Except that she wasn't looking at that particular part of his anatomy. She was looking him straight in the eye. She had beautifully expressive eyes, which at this moment were shadowed and sad, but when they had been kissing and touching and exploring each other's bodies, when she had revealed how gloriously, sensationally sexy she could be, they had turned into golden orbs. She had wanted him as much as he had wanted her.

Now it looked as though he would have to be patient, very patient.

Elena sighed. Vidal was making her feel uncomfortable. This was a side to him that she hadn't been aware of. He was actually being nice and, although she appreciated the fact that he hadn't forced her into making love, she knew that it still wouldn't do to trust him completely.

He was too virile a man to go without his pleasure, nor was she sure that she would be able to resist him the next time. Her inability to go on had probably been a psychological block, caused by the trauma of the day.

Amazingly, even now she felt like flinging herself back into his arms, declaring that she was ready—but knew that it would be far too embarrassing if the same thing happened again.

On the other hand she could not see Vidal accepting twelve whole months of nothingness, despite what he had said.

Actually she ought to be thanking Vidal, not backing off. If he hadn't agreed to marry her and take over their bank then her mother would be in a far worse condition. She had clearly worried herself sick over the last few months. And now that a heart murmur had been discovered they must all pull together and see that she had no more serious concerns. If only her parents had said something before. Not that she personally could have saved the bank, but she might have been able to do something.

Instead of putting herself into the hands of Vidal Marquez!

'I am grateful to you, Vidal,' she conceded reluctantly. 'Without your help my mother might not—' Tears filled her eyes and she dashed them away angrily. 'My mother could be a lot worse. I never knew how bad things had got and how worried both she and my father were.'

Vidal felt sorry for Elena's mother too, very much so, and he knew that she didn't need any more stress, but he didn't want to talk about her now. On his wedding day! When he should be partaking in glorious sex. Where was the fairness in this world? The way he looked at it, making love would help take Elena's mind off her mother. And it would certainly help him.

Marrying her wasn't having the result he had expected. From the instant he had set eyes on the newly grown-up and deliciously exciting Elena he had wanted her. He'd said that he was prepared to wait—but hell, he wasn't made out for the waiting game. Especially when she'd responded so amazingly.

He smiled slowly. 'The pleasure will wait. I can be patient. Though I'm afraid that for tonight we'll still have to share the same bed.'

Elena knew very well that his smile wasn't genuine. She also knew the impossibility of Vidal sharing a bed and doing nothing. But what choice had she? There was a sofa in the adjoining room, but it was overstuffed and not conducive to a good night's sleep. Not that she expected to get any sleep—even in the bed. How could she with Vidal at her side? He was too magnetic, too potent, too everything.

In the end she did slide into the bed, pulling her negligee tightly around her, conscious of Vidal's still naked body only inches away. She lay a long time listening for his breathing to deepen, conscious of the heat of his body, conscious too of the uneven pulsing of her heart. This was the hardest thing she had ever done. But once he was asleep then she too closed her eyes and drifted into unconsciousness.

Vidal could not believe that he had slept with a woman and not made love to her. Especially on his wedding night. What sort of a fool was he? Wasn't he man enough to have persuaded her into letting down her defences? He didn't blame her for what had happened, even though he couldn't truly understand it, but perhaps he ought to have coaxed and teased her into submission.

Why had he let her get away with it? This was like nothing he had ever done before.

He'd woken just as dawn was breaking and stood a few moments looking down at Elena. In sleep her face was relaxed, the early-morning light touching her with an ethereal softness. She looked like an angel, her dark hair tousled as though she had spent the night tossing and turning, a faint smile on her lips. Maybe she was dreaming a beautiful dream. Maybe she was dreaming that he was making love to her!

The thought caused everything inside him to tighten. *Dios*, how he wanted her!

She had already given away the fact that he had the power to arouse her—beautifully. All that had stopped her letting him make love last night had been her conscience. What he needed to do now, if he wasn't to spend the next year sleeping alone, was to persuade her that everything would be okay.

But he would be patient, he would let her come to him in her own good time. Not that he wouldn't try a little gentle persuasion. What fun would there be in being married otherwise?

By the time he had showered and dressed Elena was awake. She looked at him shyly as she got out of bed and he wondered whether he was the first man she had ever slept with. It made him realise how little he knew about her. And he surprised himself by wanting to know more.

He had thought, when he had agreed to their marriage, that it would simply be a case of them sharing a bed. It was the only direction his thoughts had gone. He had wanted her body and wasn't interested in her for any other reason. But now, conversely, he wanted to find out every single thing about this woman who was giving up her life to help her parents.

'Good morning, Elena. How are you feeling?'

Her finely shaped brows shot up, as though she hadn't expected such courtesy. She pulled her robe more tightly around her. 'I'm well, thank you. I'd like a shower.'

'Of course.' His stomach muscles tightened. He wasn't used to fully clothed women this early in a morning. Usually they were more ready to disrobe than cover up. And he certainly wasn't used to someone who looked as though she would prefer to be anywhere but in the same room as him.

'Meanwhile I'll order breakfast,' he said, aware that his tone was suddenly curt and despising himself for it. But how did she expect him to behave when he had spent the night next to her in bed?

He wasn't made of stone—though at this moment he wished that he were. And when Elena rejoined him a few minutes later, her damp hair clinging to her cheeks, her velvet-soft skin flushed, her wide golden eyes troubled, he wanted to take her into his arms and assure her that everything was going to be all right.

CHAPTER SIX

'THIS is where you live?' Elena queried, her beautiful eyes even wider than ever as Vidal drove through the electronically controlled gates of an impressively styled manor house.

Her parents' house was luxurious, and her own place in LA was pretty smart, but this—well, it surprised her by its size. It was twice the size of his father's house, tucked into the Andalucian countryside, a huge square two-storey property with stables and outbuildings and even what looked like a separate cottage.

Why would one man live in a place like this? she asked herself. Unless, of course, he did a lot of entertaining—in which case it would certainly be good for his image.

'And yours for the duration of our marriage.'

Elena hadn't realised that Vidal was watching the changing emotions on her face and when her eyes met his, when she heard the earthy growl in his voice, she felt a flood of something she would rather not think about.

'Well—what do you think of it?' Vidal's voice penetrated her thoughts.

'It's bigger than I expected.'

He nodded. 'I like space. I like room to move around.'

It certainly looked as though he had that. 'Do you entertain a lot?'

'Not frequently,' he answered with a shrug, 'but I do host the occasional party. We must have one while you're here. You could organise it if you like.'

Elena threw him a quick glance of protest. 'Aren't you running away with yourself? You're making it sound like a proper marriage.' And it would never be that, not ever. Not even if their bodies joined in some magnificent play of hunger and greed. Which they undoubtedly would. Living together, sleeping together, it would be impossible not to share each other's bodies as well.

'Why shouldn't it be?' His lips quirked and surprising humour lightened his eyes. 'What's the point of being married and not enjoying ourselves?'

'I didn't think enjoying ourselves was the point of the exercise.' Elena heard the caustic note in her voice and winced inwardly. If she wasn't careful she would make matters worse.

'It's not too late to back out,' Vidal warned, his eyes swiftly losing their softness, turning into savage slits of silver. 'Maybe that's what you were trying to tell me last night?'

Elena shuddered as she felt the waves of his hostility wash over her. Unfortunately she needed to hold the candle to the devil. For that was what he was—a devil!

'I won't do that. I have no wish to let my parents down. I'm here to help them, not make matters worse.'

She looked straight at him as she spoke, saw a mixture of impatience and arrogance cross his face.

The next second he turned away. 'Come, let me introduce you to the staff.'

Indoors, in the vast entrance hall they were already lined up waiting to meet her. The housekeeper, his head cook, various maids, his secretary, his personal valet and finally the gardener and his assistant. Even the stable boys.

It was an impressive line-up of staff and Elena could not believe that he needed so many. On the other hand it was a large house to keep and the gardens were vast so she guessed that they all had their duties.

As she shook hands with each one in turn she was conscious of being studied as she had never been before. What would they think if they knew that theirs was a temporary marriage? Would they look at her with such respect then? Or would they talk and sneer behind her back?

They must certainly be wondering why he had married her instead of Reina. Her sister would be well-known to them. How tongues must have wagged when she'd reneged on their marriage. Not that it would bother Vidal. He would rise above it—as she must if she were to create the right impression.

His housekeeper spoke. 'Shall I take your new wife upstairs, Señor Marquez?'

'Thank you, Marita, but I will do it myself.'

Everyone silently disappeared and Vidal smiled at Elena. 'I think you've created quite an impression. I've never seen such awe on their faces.'

'I expect they were wondering what had happened

to Reina,' she declared with a flash of her magnificent eyes. 'And I think it was curiosity rather than awe.' Although she privately thought that it was Vidal himself they feared. He was very much the lord and master.

She followed him up the grand curved staircase to a room that was massively oversized. It had parquet flooring and a monster-sized bed and was decorated richly in shades of gold and ivory. Leading off it was a sitting room, which he said she could have for her own personal use, and through another door were two bathrooms, all gold and marble with monogrammed towels.

There were two dressing rooms as well. Vidal flung open the door to one that was totally empty. 'Plenty of space for your belongings,' he declared airily, and Elena noticed that her suitcases had already been brought up.

She couldn't help wondering, however, who had used it before her. Before her sister even. She couldn't imagine Vidal living in this big space alone. Unless he used another bedroom when he was alone here? Maybe this one had been designed especially for when he took a bride. Or for when he entertained his lady friends! The thought of some other woman sharing that bed with him turned her stomach.

'Shall we continue the grand tour?'

Elena shrugged. 'As you wish.'

Her careless response dragged his brows together in a fierce frown. 'You don't sound very enthusiastic.'

And *he* sounded angry! Which didn't surprise her considering that he had spent the night sleeping with her, but not touching her. How hard must that have been for him? Practically impossible, she guessed.

And the next second she found out how impossible

it had been. 'I cannot do this, Elena,' he growled. 'I know I promised, but you have no idea what you're putting me through. I want you in my bed and in my arms! And if you'd only relax I believe you want me too.'

Elena closed her eyes, trying to shut out the vision of Vidal's face contorted with frustration. He was so right. She did want him. But she was scared now in case it happened again.

In the end she was given no choice. Vidal's arms were around her, his mouth taking possession of hers in a kiss that declared war. In a kiss that took her breath away and left her reeling. 'Forget that this is a temporary marriage,' he insisted. 'Forget the barriers. *Believe* that I am your husband. Come to me. Give me your body, let me make love to you.'

Elena did not answer; how could she when his mouth had returned to hers? When he was filling her with sensations that felt like electrical impulses? Her whole being had become intensely, magnificently alive. He had switched her on with the ease of a skilful lover.

From deep within her throat came a sound of exquisite pleasure and she could not stop herself kissing him back, her lips parting willingly to allow his tongue the access he demanded. She heard the deep guttural groan deep down in his throat as he tasted and explored, his arms binding her to the hard strength of his body.

Fireworks exploded inside her head, her hands clutching, her fingers threading through the wiry thickness of his hair. The scent of him in her nostrils nearly drove her crazy, and when she urged her body closer to his the force of his desire shocked her.

Instead of pulling away, though, she allowed herself

to be carried along on a tide of passion. Feelings that she had never expected to experience where this man was concerned were blossoming and swelling and threatening to overtake her.

It was like a roller-coaster ride of passion. The short heart-stopping ride to the first peak before a swift rush of adrenaline as she was plunged headlong into one electrifying experience after another.

Each kiss, each touch of his fingers as he explored her breasts, finding the hard, sensitive nub of each one that sprang into life the second he touched her, each time she felt his hardness against her, all conspired to whisk her into a world where nothing was real, where senses were the order of the day. Into a world she had entered with no other man.

There was no doubt about it. She wanted him to make love to her. And this time she vowed that nothing would stop her, not even her own built-in defences. She wanted this man with a fervour that should have shocked her but didn't, a fervour that carried her along on a tide of emotion too big to deny.

She therefore felt a sense of acute disappointment when he suddenly released her. How could he call a halt when he was the one who had started this? How could he deny what his body wanted? What both of their bodies hungered for?'

'Vidal,' she protested, trying to hold onto him.

'Shh, *mi amor*.' He touched a light finger to her lips. 'I hear footsteps approaching. But I promise you—' his lips curved meaningfully '—that this is not the end. Later, when we're settled in. When your maid has un-packed and—'

'*My* maid?' she asked, her voice full of shock.

'Naturally. She will look after you well. You only have to ask and she will—'

'But I don't want someone doing things for me. I'm perfectly capable of doing everything for myself. Heavens, anyone would think you were royalty!'

He frowned. 'I am a busy man—I thought you understood that. I race from one meeting to another, from one country to another. It's appropriate that I have my needs catered for.'

'Maybe you, but not me,' she declared fiercely. 'I can look after myself, thank you very much. If you'd kindly tell your staff that then—'

'Elena!' The warning in his voice silenced her and she turned wide golden eyes up to his face. 'This is the way I live. This is the way you will live. You'd better get used to it.'

The moment of passion had gone. The old arrogance was back. Vidal turned and walked out of the room and seconds later her personal maid entered.

Elena did not see Vidal again for a few hours, which was probably just as well because his comments had infuriated her. *This is the way I live. This is the way you will live. You'd better get used to it.* How dared he speak to her like that? Why had she let him? Why hadn't she come back with some equally smart retort?

The answer was simple. She was doing this for her mother. She did not want to see her in hospital again and needed to keep a hold on her tongue, which was something she was not used to doing. And she certainly hadn't realised what she would be expected to put up with. It was no wonder her sister had wanted out.

Elena spent the day exploring the house, finding her way around, talking to the various members of staff who were all extremely friendly, if guarded, and no one said anything to make her fearful that they would question what had happened between Reina and Vidal.

She walked around the gardens too. In LA she'd lived in an apartment so it was enviable to have so much open space. There were fruit trees—figs, oranges, lemons, limes, avocado and many more. There was even a hundred-year-old carob tree, according to the gardener, in the middle of one lawn. And a round pavilion—although she wasn't sure what purpose that served. Perhaps to sit in to escape the rays of the sun?

Stopping by the stables, she made friends with the horses, in particular a magnificent black stallion that she was told was Vidal's own personal horse. According to his groom no one else was allowed to ride him.

Elena used to ride before she went to America, she and Reina each having their own horses, and she was very tempted to take out the stallion. Even if only to annoy Vidal. But perhaps not today.

Her biggest find was the swimming pool and its assortment of terraces and seating areas. It beckoned to her like a consuming force and she hurried back indoors to don her swimsuit, happy that she had brought one with her.

And it was here that Vidal found her. He watched unobserved from beneath a tree as Elena swam several lengths. Her long, lazy, graceful movements tempted him to remain in the shadows rather than join her. She was taller and slimmer than her older sister and he found it constantly hard to believe how much she had changed from the scrawny schoolgirl who had held no interest for him whatsoever. If anything she had been an annoying little nuisance, hanging around when he had wanted to be with her sister.

His stomach muscles tightened as he strove to clamp down on his hunger for her now and he promised himself that she wasn't going to get away from him tonight. Never had a woman held him in such thrall.

Even if circumstances had been different, if she had been a complete stranger, he would have looked at her once, twice, and then again. He would have made it his duty to find out who she was. He would not have been satisfied until he had pursued and bedded her.

His heart thudded heavily against his ribcage at the very thought of her sharing his bed tonight and he intended making sure this time that nothing happened to stop them—not even Elena herself. He stepped out of the shadows and as he did so, as if she had sensed him, she looked his way.

'You found the pool, I see.' He kept his tone soft and unchallenging, feeling himself drowning in the wide golden orbs of her eyes. Had she always had such gorgeous eyes? Why had he never noticed before? He wanted them close to him; he wanted to look deeply into them, preferably in bed, with her arms and her legs wrapped around him.

'You should have told me about it. It's heaven in here.' She turned on to her back and began kicking lazily away from him.

If it wasn't an invitation to join him then he didn't know what was. Urgently stripping down to his shorts, he dived cleanly into the water, coming up underneath her so that she gave a tiny scream as he rolled her into his arms.

'You swim like a mermaid, Señora Marquez,' he murmured in her ear. 'And you look just as enchanting.' He dropped a light kiss onto her lips, pulling back again quickly before she could object.

'And you, Señor Marquez, should take more care of your clothes.'

He frowned and then followed the direction of her eyes. His trousers and shirt that he had thrown off so hastily were floating in the water a few feet away.

'That, my beautiful wife, is because I couldn't wait to join you.' The sight of her half-naked body was driving him insane. 'Have you ever been made love to beneath the water?' The words were out before he could stop them. And he held his breath as he waited for Elena's answer.

She looked at him for many long seconds before laughing. 'I would assume it's a physical impossibility.'

'Would you care to prove it?' he challenged, keeping his voice light.

'Maybe if ours was a real marriage then I would.' There was a glint of mischief in her amazing liquid-gold eyes that made him draw in a swift and uneven breath. 'But since it's all make-believe I'll decline the offer, thank you. Especially as I can see your gardener heading towards us.'

Vidal cursed beneath his breath. Elena was right. Marcelo was marching determinedly their way. For once in his life Vidal wished that he lived alone—entirely alone. Then he could make love to the magnificent Elena all day long if he so wished.

Maybe they *should* have gone away on honey-moon—except that only today he had received further reports on her parents' bank and they were not good. Immediate action was necessary if a catastrophe was to be avoided.

Elena did not know whether to be sad or sorry that Vidal's gardener needed to speak to him. The more they were together, the more he turned her on, the more she felt that her body wouldn't let her down a second time. She wasn't in love with him or anything stupid like that, it was simply that he had the most amazingly toned body, and the most charismatic eyes she had ever seen.

His eyes told her a lot, even though he might not know it, turning a whole different range of greys according to his mood. She hadn't learned all of them yet, but she was getting there. They had already gone from tempered steel to erotic silver. One end of the spectrum to the other. One end of his mood swings to the other. It would be interesting to find out what happened in between.

Vidal's conversation with his gardener lasted so long that Elena grew tired and climbed out of the pool, striding decisively towards the changing rooms she had spotted earlier. She was conscious of the men's conversation stopping, conscious too of Vidal's eyes watching her—so she walked that little bit taller, swaying her hips, behaving like the siren she had never been before.

What had got into her she didn't know, nevertheless it felt good. She was actually beginning to feel like a different person here. As though a temptress had climbed inside and taken her skin. It felt wickedly decadent. Perhaps this was the way to play the part? The only way she could cope with marriage to a man she did not love?

Elena was in the middle of showering when she sensed Vidal's approach. His footsteps were silent, but the air changed. It thickened and she froze, stilling her movements.

He did not call her name, he simply appeared.

In the shower with her!

Stark naked!

'What are you doing?' she squeaked when he slid his arms around her waist and pulled her hard against him. Thighs against thighs, the roughness of his chest hairs against the softness of her breasts. The hardness of his erection against her pelvis. Elena wasn't sure whether to protest or enjoy.

She was given little option when the next second a firm, long-fingered hand cupped her chin and turned her face up to his where his waiting lips greedily captured hers.

'Mmm,' he groaned deep in his throat, thrusting one thigh between hers. 'You taste divine, Elena.'

As did he! He tasted of male hunger, and he promised hot sex. Which meant she either got out now—or not at all.

Unconsciously she moved her body closer, feeling his hard maleness against her own softer femininity, and in that moment of weakness the decision had been made for her. Of their own accord her lips parted, her head falling back on her shoulders, and nothing mattered now except the power and passion, the strength and sensuality that Vidal wielded over her.

'Not only do you taste good, but you feel good, *mi amor*.'

His voice was little more than a growl and Elena responded with a groan of her own. It took her several more seconds to realise that he was no longer kissing her.

He was not even touching her!

She opened her eyes, at first seeing nothing but hot glittering silver, but when she took in the wider view she realised that his legs were braced and his hands were on the wall either side of her. She was in a human cage where to move was to touch him, where not to move was swiftly becoming torture.

Water coursed across his back and along the tensed muscles of his arms, running down his magnificent torso, flattening his dark chest hairs, making her want to touch, to stroke, to feel his strength—but there was something strangely taboo about it at this moment.

He was the captor, she was his prisoner. He was the dominant male. She was his to play with as he liked. And heavens, did she want him to play with her. Every female hormone that she possessed was clamouring for release, and the longer he stood there not touching, the more potent they became.

'Vidal…' she whispered tentatively.

'Vidal, what?'

The question came from somewhere deep in his throat and Elena fancied that she could feel the vibration. A further tremor shivered through her limbs. 'Nothing,' she managed, shaking her head, wanting to turn her eyes from his, but they were held there by a magnetic force over which she had no power.

'Were you perhaps asking me to kiss you—like this?' With his eyes still holding hers he stroked gentle fingers down her cheek, tracing her shape with inconceivable slowness, creating a whole host of sensations, before trailing those same incredibly knowing fingers at a snail's pace down the arch of her throat, pausing on the fluttering pulse at its base, exploring its erratic beat before returning to tip up her chin.

His face came down to hers like a dark angel, fear and excitement threatened to overspill, and Elena could contain herself no longer. She met his lips with an eagerness she feared regretting later. Hunger took over. Vidal had created a storm inside her—one that only he could assuage.

'You are aware of where this kiss will lead?' His hoarse voice pulsed against her mouth. 'You are prepared? Because there'll be no backing out this time. You'll be my wife, my woman, totally and completely.'

Elena hardly took in what he was saying. His touch, the powerful feel of his lips, had drugged her, made her insensitive to everything except the feel of him against her hungry body. She wanted more than his kisses, she wanted him inside her. Now! No man had ever driven her to such hunger before. It was almost unbearable.

'I'm yours,' she whispered.

The groan in Vidal's throat echoed triumphantly in the enclosed space. His kiss burned into her senses, creating a crescendo of feelings that threatened to explode. The fact that they were in the shower was forgotten, she hardly felt the harsh jets of water pounding their bodies.

Vidal's lips against hers, Vidal's tongue tasting and inciting, they were her world. Vidal's hands now drawing her close to him, urging her against the exciting hardness of his arousal. Sending her as high as if she were on drugs.

Elena felt as though she had been elevated into a world reserved for senses only. An ethereal world where the human form was banned, where feelings and pleasure were the order of the day. She felt weightless and mindless and when Vidal's strong fingers splayed across her bottom, lifting and urging her over him, when he entered her with incredible gentleness—making sure there was no barrier this time—every sane thought disappeared.

Sensations such as she had experienced with no man before spun through her, contorting her limbs, making her grip Vidal's shoulders so hard that she expected her nails might draw blood.

Vidal's thrusts grew more urgent with every second that passed. She dared open her eyes to look into his face and saw that he was as far gone as she was. His eyes were glazed, his mouth almost grim. Then even as she watched his expression changed, his face screwed into agony—and she could look no more.

She too was experiencing the same painful explosion of feelings. They screamed through the part of her that he had made his own. They filled her with golden light and sparkling stars and a need to keep him thrusting against her. Wave after wave of intense emotional feelings shuddered through every inch of her.

It was all and more than she had expected from Vidal's lovemaking. If this was what marriage to him was going to be like, then perhaps twelve months wouldn't be too long after all.

CHAPTER SEVEN

VIDAL found it hard to believe that Elena had turned into such a fiery sex goddess. Earlier in the shower—when he hadn't expected it, when he had given her a get-out option even though it had killed him to offer it—she had finally given him her everything. She had responded far more fiercely, far more fully than he had ever anticipated.

Now it was the end of the day and they were in bed and had just made spectacular love again. Elena was proving insatiable, like no other woman he had met. He was a lucky man; this could have all ended so differently.

'I have to go into the office early tomorrow,' he told her gently, stroking a stray strand of hair from her forehead. 'Don't miss me too much.'

'I could come with you. You did say you could find me work.'

He looked into her soulful dark eyes. 'I did,' he agreed, 'but that was before I got to know you. I think you'll prove more of a distraction than a help and I don't want to be distracted.' He stroked a firm finger down her nose. 'Have you any idea how beautiful you are? How hard I find it to think of anything other than you here in my bed?'

When she caught his finger and pressed it to her lips, sucking it gently into her mouth, he groaned and gathered her against him again and the rest of the night passed in a blur of lovemaking and sleep.

Elena woke to find the bed at her side empty. She glanced at the clock and gave a tiny squeal. Nine-thirty! Why hadn't someone woken her? She'd had the most beautiful dream. She had dreamt that her marriage to Vidal was real and for ever. How crazy was that?

How could it be permanent when they both knew so differently? When she had been coerced into this marriage and Vidal had insisted on his conjugal rights? Why had she given in? Why did he have to be such an expert lover? Why had he made her feel as though she were special and actually meant something to him?

The problem was she'd never before had a purely physical relationship. She didn't believe in them. Maybe she was old-fashioned, but she felt that love and sex went hand in hand. Not sex for the sake of it.

And yet she was guilty of doing precisely that.

So what did it make her?

She didn't want to think about it. She sprang out of bed and hurried to take a shower, but that was a mistake because all it did was remind her of yesterday. With a swift shake of her head she towelled herself dry. What she was going to do with herself all day while Vidal was at work she didn't know. Perhaps visit her parents? See how her mother was?

In the end she decided against it, phoning instead, re-assuring herself that they were all right. And after lunch when she was sitting in the shade of one of the trees by the pool she had a visitor.

'Fernan!' More than pleased to see Vidal's brother, she flung her arms around him.

'Now there's an unexpected welcome,' he said with a grin. 'Where's Vidal? Is he around? I don't want him getting jealous.'

'He's at work,' said Elena, and there must have been something in her voice because he looked at her sharply.

'He's neglecting you already? I thought you'd at least have gone away on honeymoon?'

Elena flashed him an impatient glance. 'Don't be ridiculous, Fernan. You know the story.'

He lifted his shoulders and his dark eyes met hers. 'I know that in theory it's an arranged marriage, but you have stars in your eyes, Elena. Don't tell me you're falling for my big brother already?'

She shook her head in an explosive denial. 'There's no chance of that.'

Fernan's brows rose. He was so like Vidal: the same stature; the same level of haughtiness; the same intelligence. They were even similar-looking except that Fernan's eyes were dark brown, not the intense silver of Vidal's.

'We're getting on well,' she admitted, 'but make no mistake, everything's under control. Like I told you before, I have my own life to lead after this. I'm not letting anything interfere with that.'

'I'm glad to hear it,' he said, taking both her hands into his and smiling into her eyes. 'How's Reina, by the way? Have you heard from her?'

'Sadly, no,' answered Elena. 'I expect she'll turn up

in her own good time.' It troubled her that her sister had disappeared and no one knew where she was.

He nodded. 'I hope so, for your sake, for your family's sake. I dropped by to tell you that I'm flying to New York tomorrow. I wanted to make sure you and Vidal weren't killing each other first. Clearly you're not. Though I still think a caution is in order. My brother can be very persuasive when he sets his mind to it. Don't let yourself get drawn into something you'll later regret.'

Elena smiled. 'I can look after myself, but thank you, Fernan, for the warning. You're a good friend.'

He held her against him for a brief second. He was such a lovely, caring man that Elena could not help wondering why he hadn't been snapped up by some woman long before now.

'What the hell is going on?'

She jumped when she heard Vidal's angry voice, felt her heart flutter uneasily. 'Vidal, I didn't expect you back yet.'

'Clearly. Fernan?' His eyes were a gunmetal-grey and fiercely accusing as they settled on his brother.

Fernan shrugged and smiled and let Elena go. 'I just came to say goodbye. And to see how the newlyweds are. I'm flying out in a few hours' time.'

'Then you'd better get going,' growled Vidal.

Elena wondered whether there had always been this enmity between them or whether—and this was laughable—Vidal was actually jealous of the attention Fernan had paid her. It was ridiculous if he was. She and Fernan had always been friends, there was nothing different in their relationship. He was like the brother she had never had and always wanted.

Fernan appeared not in the least upset by his sibling's attitude. '*Adiós*, Elena. Take care. I'll see you next time I'm home.'

Elena kissed his cheek impulsively and when she looked at Vidal he was scowling again. 'What's wrong with you?' she asked, knowing full well what was going through his mind, but wanting to hear it in his own words.

'What was my brother doing here?'

'He's just told you,' she answered smartly.

'What were you doing in his arms?'

'Making love!' snapped Elena. 'What did it look like?' She couldn't believe he was asking these questions. He actually sounded jealous!

'He was kissing you.'

'He was kissing me goodbye. It's what Fernan does. We're good friends. Always have been, always will be. Satisfied?'

With a snarl he turned away and headed indoors.

Vidal had seen red when he saw his brother with Elena in his arms. He hadn't stopped to question what it meant, all he knew was that this was his woman and Fernan was taking advantage.

His woman! *Dios!* She would never be that. She was his for twelve months, and if at the end of it she wanted to get it together with Fernan there was not a thing he could do about it. Why the hell hadn't he foreseen this? They'd always been close, always the best of friends. And now that they'd met up again…

Hopefully he would have got her out of his system by the end of their contract—and then she could go with whoever the hell she liked. But until then he intended on making love to her every single day. No man would stand in his way.

If he'd ever wanted to take a punch at Fernan it had been when he saw them in each other's arms. But what would that have done to his relationship with Elena? It would have killed it stone-dead. Even if he'd insisted on them remaining married she would never have let him into her bed again. It would have been separate rooms and endless, sleepless nights.

He'd come home early with the intention of making love to his wife. He'd worked hard all day and was ready for some relaxation. Now he felt cheated. He stripped off his clothes and stormed out to the pool, punishing himself instead with lap after gruelling lap.

'Don't you think you've done enough?' Suddenly Elena was in the water in front of him, her arms outstretched along the sides of the pool. It was clear that she had nothing on and everything inside him sprang into high alert.

'Elena, get out of here.' Otherwise he would take her right where she was.

Her chin lifted in a mutinous gesture that he was beginning to recognise. This lady was not for moving, it said.

'I'm warning you, Elena.' God, she was gorgeous. It was no wonder his brother was trying to muscle in on her. And it was the thought of Fernan holding her that spurred him to launch himself at her, pulling her hard against him, pressing his lips to hers in a kiss that was both savage and seriously demanding.

Elena kissed him back, her passion as high as his, and in no time at all they hauled themselves out of the pool and ran laughing to the relative seclusion of the over-hanging branches of an olive tree.

Their lovemaking was fast and furious. Neither could get enough of each other. It was nothing but hot, sizzling sex—but what it did to him. He forgot all about his suspicions regarding his brother. Elena was his willing accomplice. She was up for anything he cared to dish out. In fact, he was the one who called a halt.

'Enough, Elena,' he declared softly, pushing himself up on his elbows. He studied her for a few minutes, 'You are amazing, do you know that? Your skin is soft and beautiful, your lips are flushed with that just-kissed look and your eyes—well, they're shining like stars. I think I'd like you in this state permanently.'

'You look very pleased with yourself, too, Señor Marquez,' she answered primly. 'Like the cat who's stolen the cream. Or should I say the stud who's found his perfect mate?'

'Mmm, I like that. My perfect mate. Is that you, Elena?' he asked softly.

'It's what I shall endeavour to be for the duration of our marriage,' she replied, her chin suddenly high, some of the softness going out of her eyes.

It had been the wrong question to ask, the wrong answer he'd been given. He wanted Elena to feel that their lovemaking was something to be enjoyed, not endured. He wanted her to enjoy it so much that she wanted more from him. He did not want her to think of it as a duty.

But perhaps she didn't. She had virtually invited him to make love earlier and it certainly hadn't felt like duty when they were in the throes of passion. He had been certain that Elena's pleasure was as great as his. So why the caustic comment?

'Do you have a boyfriend back in the States?' The words came out of nowhere. Why it had occurred to him to ask her now he didn't know.

'Of course not,' she answered swiftly, with a further flash of her magnificent eyes. 'How could I have gone through with this if I had? Do you think a boyfriend, a fiancé even, would have put up with me marrying someone else purely to save my parents' bank? Besides I've had no time for serious boyfriends.'

'Do you hate me for taking you away from your work?'

Another flash of her eyes. 'I'm not doing it for you, I'm doing it for my parents. And I don't really think we should be having this sort of a conversation when we don't have a stitch on.'

'You could wear me,' he growled, feeling himself harden all over again.

'You're getting very greedy, señor,' she returned smartly. 'I think we should get dressed and go indoors and behave like two decent adults.'

'Decent? When I'm in your company, my sweet Elena? You tempt a man beyond decency.' She was the most tempting woman he had ever met or was likely to meet. This whole affair had started out because he wanted her body, but he had discovered that there was more to Elena than he had first thought. Inside that head of hers was a keen brain and the combination was lethal.

Elena sprang to her feet and began pulling on her clothes. 'I'm merely doing the job I was asked to do.' Not for anything was she going to tell him that she enjoyed their lovemaking far more than she had ever expected. That it went a long way to making up for the fact that she'd had to put her life on hold.

Her words, however, were like waving a red rag to a bull.

'*Elena!*' There was power behind his voice and a sudden hardness in his eyes. 'I don't want you to feel like that. I want you to come to me willingly—or not at all.' He jumped up too and dragged on his trousers and shirt before storming off into the house.

What would have been his response, wondered Elena, if she'd said that she would settle for the *not at all*? His answer didn't take much working out. Nevertheless it was true—she was doing a job. Did she have to ruin things, though, by dropping it into the conversation? Or was it herself she had been reminding? Elena sighed deeply. It was proving far too easy to get carried away into believing that their marriage was for real.

And she could not afford to do that. This was a contract. Nothing more, nothing less.

Vidal kept asking himself what was wrong. Why had he gone off the deep end when Elena had said something that was perfectly true? The answer was simple. Because it reminded him that theirs wasn't a real marriage. And he didn't want reminding.

The fact that he had insisted on her marrying him in the first place no longer sat easily on his shoulders. It had seemed like a good idea at the time. He had wanted this woman beyond reason. But now that he was getting to know her, reason was beginning to step in, and he began to question whether he had done the right thing.

He had taken her away from her job and her friends

all because of his own very selfish needs—needs that were growing and expanding in a way that he had never expected. She was an incredible lover, and had given every impression that she enjoyed the intimate part of their relationship as much as he did—until she'd spoken those damning words!

So was it really all an act? *Was* it just a job to her? How would he ever know? If it was then she had to be a very consummate actress to perform the way she did. Could he demand it of her again without thinking of the words she had spoken?

This was turning into a nightmare. And he had to do something about it. He needed to persuade her that her feelings were very real. Otherwise he couldn't go through with this—charade—any longer. He did not want her to feel that she had to act when they were making love. Her words had made him uneasy and it was not something he was used to.

'I thought we would eat out tonight,' he said when she eventually returned to the house. 'At a favourite restaurant of mine, which I feel sure you will enjoy.'

Elena's smile was weak and definitely not enthusiastic, even wary perhaps, which made him wonder whether he was doing the right thing. They needed time together, though. Somewhere on neutral ground where they could relax and she wouldn't feel that she was being led into an even deeper and darker corner.

When Elena came back downstairs an hour later his heart did a strange leap. She looked amazingly beautiful in a soft amethyst dress that clung to her curves in all the right places and sent dark arrows of need through his groin. All of a sudden he didn't want to dine out, he wanted to rip the dress off and ravish her until they both ran out of energy.

Of course he did nothing of the kind. He smiled politely. 'You look stunning, Elena. Shall we go?'

Elena tried her hardest to remain distantly polite, but it lasted for less than five seconds. Vidal was the most amazing lover and after such intimacy how could she ignore him? Her feelings scared her if the truth were known. Scared her to death. But it was surely better this way than to have to suffer a sexual relationship that did nothing for her? It had been wrong to say she was doing a job, because there was no way on this earth that making love with Vidal could be called a job.

It was a pleasure.

A sheer, insatiable pleasure.

While she had been showering and getting ready to go out Elena had told herself that relaxing and enjoying the time she spent with Vidal was the only way to get through the coming year. Fighting him would be pointless. She would always be the loser, he was too gut-wrenchingly sexy to ignore.

Her nerve ends were sensitised when he took her elbow and carefully helped her into the waiting limousine. She felt as though there were a time bomb inside her waiting to go off. It was a strange, inexplicable feeling. And Vidal was adding to it by being so attentive.

Thankfully it was but a short ride to the restaurant, which was elegant and historic and one she had never been to before. With grand architecture and original features, it had a rarefied hushed atmosphere so that she felt compelled to talk in whispers.

'This is beautiful,' she said as Vidal indicated that they wished to be shown straight to their table. Was it coincidence that it was in an alcove that set them apart from other diners? She swept the thought away. Vidal clearly wanted this evening to be special so she mustn't question his choice.

It wasn't about angering him again, it was about building bridges, getting to know each other better. At least that was what she assumed Vidal had in mind. In his house with his staff always hovering it was difficult to get any real solitude. Except in bed, of course, but they had other things to occupy their minds then.

The light from the candles lent an added glow to his smooth olive skin, created a mysterious element to the silver of his eyes, and Elena sensed a different man here. Not someone who had taken her as part payment for the bank, but someone who actually cared. Someone who wanted her to enjoy this evening for what it was.

It was an odd feeling, one that she had never expected to experience with Vidal. Up until now he'd only ever wanted sex from her. It had been his enduring passion. Not that she was complaining, she enjoyed it too. But tonight looked like being something special.

'What are you thinking?' Vidal's deep, attractive voice penetrated her thoughts.

'What a beautiful place this is,' she answered.

'You've not been here before?'

Elena shook her head. 'I take it you have. Is this your usual haunt?'

'It's a place for special occasions, for special people,' he answered, his voice dropping into a low growl that sent a shiver down Elena's spine.

'You're saying that I am special?' she asked with sudden daring.

'*Naturalmente!* You are very special to me, Elena.'

It was on the tip of her tongue to say that of course she was since he was getting what he wanted, but she did not wish to spoil their evening when he had gone to so much trouble. Had he felt guilty when she had shot her earlier jibe at him? Was this his way of making her feel better about their situation?

Her thoughts were interrupted by an attentive waiter and for the next few minutes as they studied their menus they were silent, though Elena was aware of Vidal constantly slanting a glance her way.

His vigilance made it difficult for her to concentrate and in the end she closed her menu. 'You order for me,' she said huskily.

Vidal's smile told her that he was completely aware of her turmoil and she did not even listen as he gave the waiter their order. Instead she sat back and sipped her aperitif—an excellent white Rioja that had appeared at the snap of Vidal's fingers.

Gradually she began to relax and at Vidal's prompting she told him how she had started up as a wedding planner.

'I used to help out a friend,' she told him. 'When she was suddenly taken ill she asked me to look after things. Unhappily her illness was more serious than was at first thought and when it became clear that she wouldn't be able to return to work I bought her business. I had to take out a loan but I've long since paid that back.'

'So you've become a very successful lady?' Vidal sat

back in his chair, wine glass in hand, lazily studying her. 'How long have you been running your business now?'

Why did he have such beautiful eyes? thought Elena. They could never be ignored. At this moment they were sending a smouldering message, one that ignited inside her stomach, setting a trillion sense buds into motion.

'Just over five years. I'm quite well established.'

'And this assistant of yours—Kate did you say her name was? Will she protect your interests?'

'Absolutely.'

'Will you need to fly home periodically to make sure?'

Elena's brows rose. 'You would allow that?'

'Infierno,' he laughed. 'I am not such a terrible man, Elena! Of course you must go if you are needed.'

Elena could not believe what she was hearing. This was a different side to Vidal. Perhaps she ought to have told him all this in the very beginning—then he might not have insisted on their marriage. He might have found it in his heart to help her without all this nonsense.

And pigs might fly!

She had taken him by surprise and he'd had little choice but to say what he had. She doubted he'd let her go. He had made it very clear that she was his and his alone for the next twelve months. Nevertheless she said, 'That is very generous of you, Vidal.'

'So whose weddings have you organised? Anyone I might know?'

Elena shrugged and named one or two film stars he might have heard of.

'Does anything ever go wrong?'

'Oh, yes,' she answered with a laugh. 'I remember

when the bride caught her heel in the back of her wedding dress as she got out of the car at the church. She was in floods of tears especially as the hole was at the back for everyone to see. Thank goodness I had my emergency repair kit with me. A few judiciously sewn on silk flowers did the trick.'

Vidal's eyebrows rose, though he said nothing. He continued to sit quietly and listen, a faint smile playing on his beautifully moulded lips.

'And then there was the occasion when the groom never turned up.' Elena rolled her eyes at the memory. 'It transpired that his car had taken him to the wrong church because of a relief driver at the last minute. The bride was in floods of tears, even I felt panicky. But we tracked him down and all was well in the end.'

'And here was I thinking what a cushy little number it was, Elena. You have my admiration.'

'There are lots more things I could tell you about. I could sit here all night.'

Vidal smiled. 'We have the time,' he said softly.

His first genuine smile, thought Elena. He looked more relaxed than she had ever seen him; she had even forgotten her own unfortunate situation. She felt comfortable in his presence now, and when their first course arrived she ate the grilled eggplant in tomato vinaigrette with sheer enjoyment.

She was surprised when their plates were cleared away and Vidal tossed a business card onto the table in front of her.

'What's this?' she asked with a faint frown.

'You made an impression. Andres—you remember Andres at our wedding? His daughter is getting married later in the year and he'd like you to plan it. I wasn't sure that I wanted you to do it, but having listened to you now, heard your professionalism, I believe it is something you might enjoy, something for you to do while I'm at work.'

Elena studied the card and then looked back at her husband. 'You wouldn't mind?' Andres Francia was head of a big business corporation. Money would be no object, she could pull out all the stops. It was a fantastic opportunity.

'So long as it doesn't interfere in *our* time,' he answered, his brows rising, telling her as clearly as if he had spoken the words that every moment he was home he expected her to spend it with him. Quite possibly in bed.

'I'd make sure that it didn't.' Elena allowed a tiny smile to turn up the corners of her lips, deliberately making herself sound demure. While inside she was trembling with excitement. This could be the start of something much bigger. Maybe even the potential to expand into Europe!

'Perhaps you might even settle back here? I'm sure this won't be the first offer you'll get.'

'Perhaps not,' she answered with a faint smile, a happy smile. 'But I like it in LA. It is my home now. I have no wish to come back here permanently.' Not even if there was someone as fantastic in bed as Vidal. She could live without him quite easily.

Couldn't she?

It was doubtful she would find such a skilful lover elsewhere, but that wasn't what life was all about. She had been perfectly happy until now. And would be again.

And why was she thinking like this when she had the rest of the year to get through?

She actually felt sad when the evening came to an end. Every course had been perfect, Vidal's company couldn't be faulted, and they had got to know each other much better. She even nestled her head on his shoulder during the drive home and was pleasantly surprised when all he did was drop a kiss to her brow and drape his arm across her shoulders.

As far as she was concerned it was the end of a perfect evening.

Except that Vidal was not yet finished with her. When they went to bed his kisses were more passionate than ever. They spoke volumes, told her how hungry he was for her body.

It had been simmering all night. Even though he had kept his hands off her, his eyes had given him away. She wondered whether he had any idea how they darkened when he was aroused.

Neither of them wore anything when they slept— there had never been any need because whatever she had on, no matter how minuscule, he always ripped it off with hungry, impatient hands.

Now his head moved lower so that he could suckle her breasts, nipping and teasing her nipples until she squirmed with delight, while his hands explored and aroused the other part of her body that demanded his attention.

Her whole being became a mass of incredible sensation, intensified a thousandfold when he brought her time and time again to the brink of insanity. He asked for nothing himself, he was intent only on pleasuring her—and how he did that!

Inside her everything was dancing, bursting to get out. She felt as if the merest prick of the finest needle on her skin would release her feelings, they would escape to dance joyfully in the air. She fancied that she would actually be able to see her pleasure right there in front of her eyes. It would be full of light and beauty and she would never want to let it go.

Her fingernails clawed Vidal's back and she called out his name in agonised delight until he was able to hold back no longer. He took her then, not once but several times, until they both collapsed in exhaustion, swiftly followed by sleep.

When morning came Elena found the bed beside her empty and she wondered if it had all been a beautiful dream. A figment of her imagination. Wishful thinking on her part.

Then her bedside phone rang. 'Good morning, Elena.'

'Vidal, where are you?'

'I'm at the office. I wanted to check you were okay.'

And why wouldn't she be? He'd made love to her before and left without bothering to check her welfare. Why this time? But she knew the answer. Last night had been special, different. Whether it was her imagination or not Elena felt that something had changed in their re-lationship.

'I've just woken,' she said, adding more shyly, 'I missed you.'

She heard a sigh the other end and immediately knew that she had said the wrong thing, read the wrong signals. None of this was supposed to be serious. It was an affair and they were both free to walk at the end. No commitment.

'I've been called away, Elena. I'll be gone three days. If you want to return to LA to check on things there, feel free. Nevertheless I shall want you home when I get back.'

As suddenly as the phone had rung it went dead and Elena was left looking at the receiver as if she could actually see his face.

CHAPTER EIGHT

ELENA was wickedly angry that Vidal had ended their phone call so abruptly. *I'll be gone three days. Do what you like in my absence, but make sure you're there when I get back.*

Or something like that. He made it sound as though all she was good for was a bed partner. Damn the man. He had ruined every warm feeling in her body. He had cut her down to size as efficiently as if he had used a knife.

She had half a mind to go to LA and *not* come back. Why should she let him get away with it? He couldn't dictate to her like this, could he? Who did he think he was? The trouble was he had her over a barrel and he knew it. Her mother's health was at stake here. It was a case of grinning and bearing it and putting up with whatever he wanted to dish out. She had no other choice.

He was an overbearing, pompous swine and she hated him. She ought never to have succumbed to his advances. She ought never to have agreed to share his bed, insisting on separate rooms. Except that then he wouldn't have gone ahead with the merger.

Everything came back to one thing.

She shared his bed and he helped her family.

That was it. Full stop. No getting out of it. She was stuck with him whether she liked his attitude or not. Twelve months sounded like a lifetime. A prison sentence.

She phoned Kate in LA, who assured her that everything was under control and there was no need for her to come home.

Then she visited her parents. 'You look down, my darling,' said her mother, eyeing her critically. 'Is the marriage too much of an ordeal for you? I know we—'

'It's fine, *Mamá*.' Not for the world would she let them know the anguish Vidal was putting her through. It would break their hearts. 'Vidal's gone away on business for a few days.'

'But he is looking after you?' enquired her father anxiously.

Elena nodded and pasted a smile on her lips. 'He's the perfect gentleman.' She wasn't about to tell her parents that he wasn't a gentleman in bed. These were the sort of details they would not want to hear. They were under the impression that the marriage was in name only and would be horrified if they knew what their daughter got up to. If she and Vidal were in love it would be different, but under the circumstances...

'Your father and I, we worry about you. We know you're doing this for us, but Vidal's a good man.'

'Of course he is, *Mamá*, he wouldn't have offered to help you otherwise. And guess what.' She made herself sound excited. 'He's been approached by someone who wants a wedding planned. Which means I'll have something to do while Vidal's at work. I'm going to ring the guy when I get home.'

'That's wonderful news,' said her mother with a wide smile.

And her father's eyes filled with hope. 'Could it lead to you coming back here permanently?'

'I don't think so,' she answered with a faintly regretful grimace. She didn't want to get their hopes up. 'But if it does take off it means that I'll get home more often.'

Her parents looked at each other and smiled and Elena could see that she had set their minds at rest. And that was all that mattered.

As soon as she was home she made her phone call to Andres, who said he'd be in touch. In the meantime she spent her days swimming or riding. She also went shopping, charging everything to the card Vidal had left on her bedside table before he went away. It had surprised her when she found it, but she'd had no compunction about using it. Why should she when he was the one who had insisted on this ludicrous marriage?

Actually that wasn't really true—it was her parents who'd wanted the wedding. She was their lifeline, their loving daughter who had put her life on hold.

On the third day there was no sign of Vidal. He hadn't even phoned to see whether she was all right, or to say when he'd be back. In a fit of pique she decided to take out Vidal's stallion. He had expressly forbidden her to ride Jet, but she was in a dark mood this morning and needed to do something dangerous.

She had looked at Jet enviously many times, but the grooms always stood up for their master. Only one of them was allowed to exercise him, the tallest and stron-

gest man, and he was horrified now, but Elena was determined and there was nothing he could do to stop her.

'I'll take the blame,' she said. 'I won't let you get into
trouble, no matter what Vidal says.'

Jet was a magnificent thoroughbred and it felt like
riding the finest, most powerful horse in the world—
which he probably was. There would be nothing but the
best for Vidal. He was nothing like the pony she used
to ride, who was sedate and sometimes had to be urged
into a trot—a gallop being a very rare event.

Now, though, Elena felt as though she were flying
with the wind as she galloped alongside the river before
heading into the hills. Here she wanted to slow down,
but the horse had it in his mind to keep going, so she
gave him his rein and whooped with delight as they
sailed over fallen branches and narrow streams. Not
even stopping to think that if she fell off or had an
accident no one would know where to find her.

Vidal could not believe how much he had missed Elena.
He had thought it would be a good thing to be away for
a few days, give him breathing space; allow him to look
at things from a different perspective. But it hadn't
worked out like that. For some insane reason he had not
been able to get her out of his mind.

Especially in bed. The space beside him had felt
empty, his arms had felt empty, and when he had fallen
asleep he had dreamed about her. Hot dreams that had
resulted in him springing out of bed and taking cold
showers. Not that they had made much difference.

Elena had infiltrated his senses. She was there day
and night, in his thoughts and in his dreams, wickedly

wild, softly sensuous, a tantalising temptress, and he couldn't wait to hold her in his arms again, to take her to bed and make magical, heart-stopping love.

He entered the house now with a sense of anticipation. Already his heartbeats were quickening, his pulses racing, but to his intense disappointment and frustration Elena was nowhere to be found. He questioned the servants and no one had seen her since early that morning.

He scoured the grounds, his temper rising, and was about to go back inside and phone her parents when his head stable boy came running after him. 'Señor Marquez, your wife, she has taken Jet out,' he confessed uncomfortably. 'I tried to stop her, but I could not do so. She was very determined.'

Alarm bells rang in Vidal's head. 'But you know I allow no one else to ride him,' he roared. 'Especially a woman. What were you thinking?'

'I am very sorry, señor. But there was nothing we could do. She looked—very—capable,' he added lamely. 'She convinced me that she was a good rider.'

As if that helped, thought Vidal angrily. No one knew the vagaries of Jet as he did. The horse had a mind of its own and it was sometimes all Vidal could do to control him.

Every worst-case scenario flashed through his mind—she could have fallen and killed herself, the horse could have broken a leg, anything could have happened. He was on the verge of telling his groom that his services were no longer required when he heard the sound of a horse's hooves.

His relief was faint. Not only was his stable hand in

trouble but Elena too. She ought to have known better. His heart had raced when he discovered what she'd done, and he'd certainly have something to say to her.

He had come home eager to see her again, more eager than he should have been under the circumstances, and found—what? That she had taken his priceless stallion on a joyride. If anything had happened to his horse…

Or Elena!

He drew in a swift uneasy breath. It didn't bear thinking about.

Elena grinned as she halted beside him. 'I didn't know you were back. What an impressive beast. How I enjoyed riding him.'

'You could have been killed,' he snarled. 'Haven't I told you never to take him out? No one rides Jet but me. He's far too strong for you to handle. You're lucky he didn't throw you.'

Her golden eyes looked innocently into his. 'He's safe and sound, what are you worrying about? Besides, we both needed the exercise,' she added as she dismounted, patting the black beauty, who nuzzled his head against her.

Vidal could not believe what he was seeing. Jet loved no one but him. He'd always been difficult to handle. And yet here he was showing affection for Elena. Damn it!

'What if you'd fallen? What if you'd hurt yourself?' he asked savagely. 'What if Jet was hurt?'

'But we weren't so you're protesting about nothing,' she retorted. 'I can't see what all the fuss is about. He's a little pussycat.' She smiled to the groom who led him away and then flared her eyes magnificently at Vidal.

'I'm going to shower and change. To think I was actually looking forward to you coming home.'

Vidal watched her as she walked away. She had the arrogance of Jet, it was there in every line of her body, the way she moved, the lift of her head—she even had the same black hair. Elena was a thoroughbred without any doubt.

Maybe he had gone over the top, but *infierno*, what if she *had* fallen? What if she'd been badly hurt? It didn't bear thinking about and he most certainly was not going to let her take Jet out again.

Perhaps it hadn't been such a good idea going away. Except that it had been very necessary. And there would be other times. Maybe it would be more expedient in future to take her with him.

He'd certainly missed her in his bed. Elena had begun to relax in his company. When she'd related those stories about weddings gone wrong he had enjoyed seeing her lighter side, warming to her more than he had ever thought possible.

He'd lain there every night unable to sleep, imagining her lithesome body next to his, the fragrance of her skin filling his nostrils, the tight feel of her as she closed around him. The delightful sounds she made when an orgasm shattered her.

Even thinking about it now made him hurry after her. He shouldn't have been so hard on her. She was safe. It was time to calm down and enjoy the delights of her body once again. It was what had driven him all day, right from the first second he awoke. His disappointment when he'd found her missing had been acute. Was it any wonder that he had flared up?

Vidal stalked through the house, memories of the time they had shared a shower, the first time he had made love to her, flooding back with a vengeance. He drew in a swift, painful breath, his body reliving that moment, recalling every tiny detail, growing hard.

He wanted that same experience again and he wanted it now!

He forgot that he had just berated her, forgot that she had marched away in anger, it didn't enter his head that she might not be willing. He began tearing off his clothes even before he reached the bedroom, leaving a trail on the floor, only slowing down when he neared her bathroom and heard Elena singing.

She had a beautiful voice. He'd never heard her sing before, and now he stood listening. It was a love song, intense and passionate with words about tasting sweetness on lips and magic every time they touched. Was she equating it to him and her, or was it just a song that she liked and held no real meaning?

He wanted it to be the former. He could equate to those words so easily. Elena's lips tasted far sweeter than any other woman he had kissed, and each time they touched, each time skin brushed against skin, there was definitely something magical in the air.

Vidal felt his breathing getting deeper and quicker and, although he knew that he mustn't rush in and demand his conjugal rights, he found himself striding far more quickly towards her than sanity declared he should do.

He was stopped in his tracks. Elena's arms were held high, her head back and her eyes closed as she sang her heart out, at the same time clearly enjoying the feel of warm, silken water streaming down her perfectly toned body.

This was temptation personified. It was almost as though she were offering herself to him. He could hear the words in his head.

Here I am, Vidal. I am yours. Yours and yours alone. Take me, take me now.

Of course he knew that this was not true, never would be true. Elena was not his, she was married to him under sufferance. She would never offer herself freely. Not that she didn't enjoy their lovemaking, but there was always a tiny part of her that held back, that reminded herself that she was under contract.

He did not want to frighten her by jumping into the shower, or even by calling out her name. So instead he began to sing the song with her, his baritone voice uniting in perfect harmony. He saw Elena go still, her voice faltering for a few seconds, until she gave a secretive smile. She didn't open her eyes, she didn't look at him; neither did she drop her arms—she simply carried on as if he were not there.

In an instant Vidal was in the shower with her, his hands on her waist. 'I never knew you could sing,' he said softly, gruffly. 'You have the voice of an angel.'

Her arms came down to drape around his neck and shoulders. 'There are many things about me that you do not know, señor.' And she slid her body sensuously against his.

It was almost his undoing.

'I'm sorry I shouted at you,' he said.

'I'm sorry I took Jet out against your wishes.'

'Shall we kiss and make up?'

'Mmm,' was the only reply he got before she stood on tiptoe and touched her lips to his.

He groaned and slid his hands around to cup her pert behind, pulling her against him. He drew in his breath in a swift whoosh of pleasure and hunger and heard Elena's similar response. Whatever else was going on in their lives, there was no doubt that making love was something they both enjoyed. Even *enjoyed* was too feeble a word. They both gloried in it—feverishly!

But remembering the time before in the shower when he hadn't stopped to use protection, Vidal now lifted her into his arms and carried her through to the bedroom, dropping her down onto the bed dripping wet. He'd been lucky that time, but he might not be so again. And complications such as a baby were definitely not on his agenda.

He was not ready to raise children. That pleasure was reserved for when he met the woman of his dreams. Someone to love unconditionally and to spend the rest of his life with. Elena was—well, Elena was Elena. This was business with a little pleasure thrown in for good measure. A lot of pleasure, actually. But in a year's time when she had fulfilled her commitment she would return to LA and he quite possibly would never see her again.

When he kissed her, though, when he sucked her nipples into his mouth, nibbling and torturing her, exulting in the little cries of pleasure she gave; when he explored the moistness between her legs, feeling her hunger, feeding it, rejoicing in her torment, in her passion, in the way she urged herself against him, Elena wasn't just Elena. Elena was a woman who had the power to satisfy him. Who held him in thrall. Who met his needs head-on with a hunger of her own. Who found equal delight in the passion they shared. Who was even getting beneath his skin in a way he had never expected. It was not going to be easy to let her go.

'I want you, Elena.' He heard his voice, deep and throaty, sounding nothing like his usual well-modulated tones, as though he were in heaven and hell at the same time. Heaven because he could feel himself floating in a sensual void that made no sense of normal, everyday feelings, a void where nothing mattered except satisfying the needs of his body. And hell because somewhere deep down in the recesses of his mind he hated himself for what he was doing. He had seen Elena as fair game in the beginning, but the more time they spent together, the more he began to respect her, the more he wished that he hadn't started this thing.

He'd been prepared to do whatever it took to make her his. And now that he had, now that he'd got to know her, found out what sort of a woman she really was, he felt angry and disappointed in himself.

Vidal dashed his thoughts away. He didn't want to go down that line, he didn't want to listen to his conscience. Elena was here, beside him, beneath him, his for the taking—what was he waiting for?

He made love slowly and beautifully, bringing both Elena and himself to the edge many times before the final, excruciating, beautifully intense moment when neither of them knew what had hit them. When their worlds were rocked and they flew into orbit before cata-pulting back to earth where they lay together in a daze of breathless surrender.

Elena woke to find herself in Vidal's arms, his fingers stroking her hair, his amazingly sexy silver eyes watchful on her face. 'How long have I been asleep?' she asked shyly. Vidal seemed different, gentler, kinder, as though she was no longer someone he had bought and intended to use, but someone he had learned to care for.

The thought stunned her—because hadn't she started to feel the same way? Had their marriage turned a corner? She was certainly happier.

But she didn't actually want him *caring* for her. Yes, she enjoyed sex with him—which was as well under the circumstances—but did she really want anything more? Vidal was not the sort of person she would ever wish to get seriously involved with.

He was a workaholic for one thing. She had already discovered how much time he spent at the office, leaving early and coming home late. She ultimately wanted children and when that happened she would want their father to be there for them.

These past three days when he hadn't been here had given her an insight into what life would be like for the woman Vidal eventually chose to be his real wife. He would be an absentee father, she felt sure. Late nights at the bank, business trips abroad. No time at all for his wife and family. If he was questioned he would say he was doing it for them, when really he was doing it for himself. It was the lifestyle he had chosen and one she doubted he would welcome relinquishing.

She knew that he was a hard man who would stop at nothing to further his ambition. He had let her and her parents think that he was doing them a favour, but in reality... She refused to let her thoughts go any further. What she must do, what was most important, was to make sure that she didn't let herself get too carried away.

'You've slept for no more than a few minutes,' he said in answer to her question, his voice soft and gentle as he continued to play with her hair.

It felt as though she'd been asleep for ages. It felt comfortable in his arms and she did not want to move. Until he began kissing her again and fierce threads of arousal began to weave their way through her body.

Swiftly she rolled away. She needed another shower, though she was not going to tell him that because she was afraid he might join her—and then the whole sequence would start all over again.

There were times when she found it hard to believe that she was letting Vidal use her body like this, although there were others when she had no such qualms. Like now, it had felt so right. They had both hungered for fulfilment and she dared not let herself think about what it actually meant or where it might ultimately lead.

It could be to heartache if she let herself get too emotionally involved. She needed to be aware at all times of what she was getting herself into. It was still nothing more than a game to Vidal, even though she had detected a subtle change in him. A game in which he was coming out the winner.

Was she a fool? Maybe, but without this chemistry between them assuming the role of Vidal's wife would have been a burden too hard to bear.

To her relief Vidal moved too. 'I don't know about

you, but all this exercise has made me hungry,' he announced with a grin. 'I'll go and see what's for lunch.'

They chose to eat out on the terrace with its amazing views over the city and surrounding area. It was a hot hazy day, the sort of day when the pool beckoned. Later, thought Elena.

Meanwhile the seafood paella was to die for. She loved shellfish of any sort and between them they ate every last shrimp, every piece of squid, every mussel. Vidal intensified her awareness of him by taking one prawn after another out of its shell and feeding them to her, slowly and deliberately, his eyes not leaving her mouth as he did so.

He had such an intense expression on his face, in his amazing silver eyes, that Elena felt a whole new whirlpool of desire. This was seduction of the worst kind. It was sheer torture. And he knew it.

Somewhere in the house she heard the phone ring. Merciful release! Vidal would be called away. She would be able to breathe again. It was amazing how the air always thickened when he was near her, when he taunted her with his presence.

But the call was not for Vidal. To her surprise the phone was brought out to her. It was Andres Francia, ready to discuss wedding plans.

'This afternoon, yes, I'm free,' she said, trying to ignore the fierce look Vidal aimed at her across the table. 'I'll see you in an hour, then.'

Vidal was furious with Elena. Hadn't he given up the whole afternoon so that he could be with her? He could have gone to the bank, in fact, he needed to be there, but no, his need for Elena had been greater.

And now she was going to meet Andres! He wished that he had never mentioned the man's name.

'You're going out?' He was aware that his voice was harsh now, devoid of all the softness when he had fed pieces of food to her across the table. He had loved the way she moistened her lips with the tip of her tongue before opening them. The way her teeth gently took each morsel of food. The way her eyes hadn't left his during the whole process.

It had been an erotic experience and he had been looking forward to spending even more time with her.

'Actually, Andres is coming here,' she announced with a slight lift of her fine brows. 'That won't be a problem, will it? I presumed you would be going to your office this afternoon?'

'Of course.' He hated the sharpness in his voice but he couldn't help himself. Didn't he always work? Did he ever take time off? It struck him now how much time he did actually spend working. On the other hand he'd never had anyone as tempting as Elena to take him away from it.

He pushed his chair back and stood up. 'In fact, I should be leaving right now.'

CHAPTER NINE

ANDRES FRANCIA was of medium height and not particularly good-looking, but he had an air of authority about him that reminded Elena of Vidal. She could not understand why Vidal had reacted so fiercely when she had announced that Andres was coming to discuss his daughter's wedding plans. The fact that Vidal had stormed away told her that he was displeased, but what was his reasoning when he was the one who had suggested she meet with Andres in the first place?

'It will be something for you to do,' he had said.

Now, when it was happening, he was annoyed. Anyone would think he had been prepared to spend the afternoon with her, when she knew perfectly well that he would have gone to the office. Did he ever take a half-day off? She did not think so.

'I expected your wife and daughter to come along with you,' she said once they were seated.

'I have no wife,' declared Andres, his thin lips pursing. 'She walked out on me when Benita was three years old.'

'I'm sorry. Will she be attending the wedding?'

Andres shrugged expressively, his hands spreading wide. 'Who is to say?'

'So you have full control. You and Benita. When will I meet her?'

'That is why I am here. I have very different ideas from my daughter. It is her wedding, yes, but I am paying. I need you to spread diplomacy.'

In other words, thought Elena, he wanted her to stand in the middle and keep the peace. It happened. Lots of parents had different ideas from their children. It would be her job to suggest something they were both happy with.

Before they had even finished discussing ideas and venues Vidal returned. Elena couldn't believe how quickly the time had flown until a glance at her watch showed her that only two hours had passed. So what was he doing back so early?

'You are still here, Andres?' His words were civil, but the tone behind them was not.

Andres seemed not to notice, but Elena most certainly did, and when the man had gone she looked furiously at Vidal. 'What's the matter, Vidal? You suggest I do this work and yet you act as though it is a crime. As though you do not approve of the time I spend with a prospective client.'

Her head was high, her eyes bright with challenge.

Vidal thought she had never looked more ravishingly beautiful. And yet he could not contain his irritation. He had watched them quietly for a few moments before making his presence known and they had seemed so cosy, sitting so close, talking so quietly, that fires had burned in front of his eyes.

What the hell is the matter with you? he had asked himself. You're acting like a jealous lover and yet you know that is not the case. Elena means nothing to you. Nothing! You're conducting an affair, that is all. You'd be as well to remember that.

'I did not expect him to be here this long,' he said now, endeavouring to keep his voice level. 'Where is his daughter? Why wasn't she here as well? It is her wedding after all.'

'I shall be meeting her,' said Elena calmly, and the very fact that she had not raised her voice frustrated him further.

'Then make sure that you do,' he answered. 'I do not trust Andres.' There, he had said it, he had said what was in his mind. And unfortunately Elena picked up on it.

'You're jealous!' she claimed with a sudden smile, a smile that lit up her whole face, that released his male hormones, that made him want to pull her hard against him and kiss her senseless.

'Yes, I am,' he agreed. How could he say otherwise when his body had hardened and he wanted her shamelessly? 'You are my girl, my woman. No other man shall have you.'

It was the strangest feeling. He had never in his life felt jealousy, never felt this searing emotion that had made him want to throw Andres out of his house. Seeing them sitting so close together, leaning so intimately towards each other, had been like a physical pain. As if someone had stabbed a knife into his heart.

Dios! What did it mean? Not that he was falling in love with Elena, surely? That wasn't possible. All he'd ever wanted was her body. She wasn't his wife in the true sense of the word. So why the hell was she bringing out this alien side to his character?

'No other man will,' she assured him, her golden eyes steady on his. 'At least not until we go our separate ways.'

Elena knew that she ought not to have tagged on these last words—except that they were a safety net against her own feelings. She watched the flicker in Vidal's eyes, saw the way his nostrils dilated, the way his mouth firmed. It all happened in a second, she could almost have imagined it. But she knew that she hadn't.

He was saying that he owned her! Body and soul. For the duration of their contract. And woe betide any other man who looked at her during that time.

But to be actually jealous of Andres, that was a different matter. Unless he was changing his mind about her? Could it be that he was beginning to feel something too? Was she getting beneath his skin? Elena dared not let her thoughts go any further. It was too improbable.

And yet...

How did she feel about him? He was a damned good lover, that went without saying, and there were times when she had actually felt they were a real husband and wife. But always she had scoffed at her own fantasy. Vidal was in it for what he could get out of it, and she'd do as well to remember that—even if her feelings towards him were changing.

A proper marriage would never work. Their life-styles were far removed. Vidal would suffocate her. He would want to bend her to his will, and that was not the sort of partner she wanted.

'That is obviously what I meant,' he declared gruffly. 'Now come here and let me kiss you.'

And stupidly she did. She couldn't help herself. As soon as his lips touched hers she forgot her fears, she forgot everything, letting herself drift into a state of heightened passion. And in bed that night heaven and earth moved again, making Elena wonder whether any other man would ever arouse her in this same seriously magical way. Was it possible? Or was Vidal the only man for her?

Vidal was late getting home. As usual he had got caught up in a business meeting, but now he couldn't wait to see Elena, to feel the warmth of her in his arms, to taste her exciting kisses, to make spectacular and satisfying love.

There had been a sudden shift in their relationship recently and he felt sad when he thought about it coming to an end. He had even, stupidly, wondered if she would ever agree to make their marriage real.

Which led to the question, was he in love with her? The answer was a resounding no. At least he didn't think so. He had actually never been in love so what did he know about such things? He was very aware that Elena had begun to get beneath his skin as no one else ever had, and the thought of losing her at the end of the year made his heart feel heavy. He had even hated seeing her talking to Andres. He had known they were talking weddings, Andres's daughter's wedding, for heaven's sake, but even so he had felt the green eye of jealousy streak into his veins.

Tonight he intended to make it up to her—again. In his mind's eye he could see her standing naked and proud

133

in front of him. She had a fantastic figure. High, firm breasts that taunted him beyond belief when her nipples grew taut, beckoning him as the sun did to the flowers.

She was slender without being thin, with softly curved hips and a flat stomach. In the apex of her thighs dark hair curled and hid from his eyes the sensitive heart of her. The part he had made his own. He sprang to life at the very thought of touching her there, making her wriggle and pretend indifference until ultimately she lifted herself up to accommodate him.

Oh, Elena, he groaned. If only you knew what you do to me.

She was waiting for him when he entered the house, wearing a white dress that he had not seen before. It was incredibly short and skimmed her curves, and looked as though it had cost a fortune—which it probably had, even though there was very little of it! He smiled wryly as he recalled his credit-card bill the other day.

But hell, it was worth it. He'd have spent it a hundred times over to see her looking so seductively tempting. If he wasn't mistaken she was wearing nothing beneath. There was no giveaway line of a bra or panties, or even a thong.

He stood for a long moment just looking at her, feeling his heart race and his testosterone levels rise so high that he thought he might burst and they would explode all over the place, letting Elena know exactly how much she taunted him.

But he would be no good to her then, so he restrained his feelings, smiling instead. 'You look good enough to eat.'

'And I expect you're worn out,' she said softly.

'You've had a long day. Marita has dinner ready so why don't you go and shower and I'll see you back down here?'

'You could join me,' he suggested, hearing the hunger in his voice.

'When I've dressed myself up especially for you?' she asked softly. 'I don't think so. I'll see you in a few minutes, Vidal.' And with that she turned and sashayed out of the room.

It was as though she was trying to convince him all over again that he had been mistaken when he'd thought Andres was coming on to her. He sang as he showered and in honour of Elena dressing up for him he pulled on a new pair of cream linen trousers and a black shirt.

Satisfied that he looked as good as she did, Vidal rejoined her downstairs. Dinner was, as usual, being served on the terrace and he found Elena out there.

'So what have you been doing with yourself today?' he asked. 'And before you answer that, may I be permitted to say how gorgeous you look?'

'You've already told me,' she said softly.

'And is it a crime to tell you again?'

'You can tell me as many times as you like,' she answered. 'A girl always likes compliments. I haven't been doing very much actually. I'm waiting to hear from Andres's daughter so that I can begin thinking about her wedding. They're at complete loggerheads about it. But really I've had a very quiet day.'

Vidal did not want to talk about Andres, or his daughter or wedding plans. He wanted to talk about Elena and this sexy new image she was portraying tonight. If he hadn't known better he would have said she was hiding a secret.

Perhaps it *was* Andres? He blanched as the thought suddenly hit him. Perhaps she had spoken to him again today. Perhaps this was what had put a lift to her step, the smile on her lips. *Dios!* He'd kill the man, he surely would.

Nevertheless he managed to keep a tight rein on his feelings.

'How was *your* day?' she asked him now. 'You looked tired when you came home.'

'All of my days are tiring,' he answered. 'But when I have someone like you to come home to it makes it all worthwhile.'

'I won't be here for ever,' Elena reminded him.

Vidal chose not to bite, smiling instead. 'Which makes it all the more important to enjoy what time we do have together.'

Their first course was put in front of them—slices of melon with smoked ham, and as she forked each delicious piece into her mouth Elena was conscious of Vidal watching her. She had the feeling that he would have liked to feed her each piece himself.

Chicken and prawns followed, a delicious dish with onions, tomatoes and garlic, but Elena could not finish it all. 'Did you know,' she asked, putting down her knife and fork, challenging one of the long dark looks he kept giving her, 'that it's my birthday next week?'

Instantly his face changed. Surprise and a smile followed. 'No, I did not. Why have you never told me?'

'Because it would look like I was angling for a present.'

'But of course you must have one,' he cut in at once. 'Do you want to tell me what you would like, or do you prefer surprises?' He lifted his glass and took a sip of his wine, looking at her speculatively over the rim. 'We must do something to celebrate. How about a party?'

'Oh, Vidal, I'd love that,' she exclaimed. It was exactly what she had been thinking herself. She needed something to relieve the tedium of days spent alone. She had dressed carefully tonight, psyching herself up to ask him, and now there was no need. 'Organising it will give me something to do. I've been—'

He silenced her with a soft finger across her lips, smiling tenderly at her enthusiasm. 'Make whatever plans you like, invite whomever you like—except Andres, of course,' he added on a warning note and much to Elena's amusement.

Elena enjoyed making the arrangements. It made her feel as though she belonged, more settled into her marriage. She had never expected to feel this comfortable or so at ease. She had fought against her feelings for Vidal and yet as each day passed she felt that she was getting closer to him. She was even beginning to feel that their marriage might work, something that would have filled her with shock and horror a few weeks ago.

Vidal had changed; he was far more loving towards her. She didn't feel any more when they made love that it was simply because he hungered for her body. She sensed a closeness, a respect even.

She invited a mixture of her own family and friends and some of Vidal's family as well.

'You're looking much happier these days,' he said over dinner one evening.

'Am I?'

'More content.'

'That's because I have something to do,' she said. 'I've always been used to a busy life. You have no idea what it's been like sitting doing nothing.' Waiting for him to return so that they could make love! The time they spent in bed was the highlight of her day, Vidal managing to turn her into someone she hardly recognised.

Never had she envisaged that she could behave so wantonly, so freely, often initiating their lovemaking herself. They became one when they were making love, each finely attuned to the other's needs. She was falling in love with him without a doubt. And she even wondered whether Vidal was falling in love with her too. Was it possible? How would she ever know?

The night of her party arrived. Fairy lights adorned the gardens, the caterers had arrived, the band had set up in the pavilion, a floor had been laid for dancing and Elena was in her dressing room getting ready when Vidal moved in quietly behind her.

She felt the hairs on the back of her neck rise when he gently touched her arms and dropped a kiss on her nape. It was a fact of life that these feelings would never go away. She wished that she could keep him at arm's length, but it was impossible. The chemistry between them was overwhelming.

'I didn't hear you coming,' she said, turning to look into his face.

'You look beautiful, *mi querida*. And I have something for you.'

Elena frowned. 'But you've already given me my

birthday present.' One that she had never expected and was outrageously expensive.

'A car.' He dismissed it as of no consequence.

But to Elena it had been the ultimate gift. A stunning sports car with cream leather seats. Her mouth had dropped open when he had taken her to see it. 'I cannot accept this,' she said immediately.

'Why not?' he asked gruffly.

'It's not right, not when our marriage isn't permanent.'

His eyes had narrowed at her reminder, but he had refrained from commenting, insisting instead that she keep it for the duration, saying that she needed some sort of transport. How he could say that when he had a garage full of cars, any of which were at her disposal, she did not know.

And now he was giving her something else! None of it made sense. What was he trying to tell her? She took the white leather box, knowing by the familiar gold logo that it was more jewellery. Determined that she was going to give it back to him, she opened the lid.

And gasped.

It was a string of very fine gold chains, each one held together with a series of tiny pearls. It was the most beautiful thing she had ever seen. It would actually go perfectly with her red dress, which had a plunging neckline and a straight calf-length skirt, split down one side to reveal an almost indecent length of leg.

She had chosen red because Vidal had once said that it was his favourite colour and some imp inside her had wanted her to be at her most tempting tonight. 'Oh, Vidal, it's beautiful,' she cried. 'I love it. Thank you so much. How do you always know what I like? Put it on for me, please.'

'It is my pleasure,' he said gruffly, but before taking the necklace out of its box he placed it down and pulled Elena into his arms. Tilting her chin, looking deeply into her golden eyes, he lowered his head and kissed her, a kiss that threatened her sanity and told her again that she was dangerously close to being in love with him.

Vidal's hormones were playing havoc. Elena looked so incredible this evening. She had a glow to her that had been missing on their wedding day, even though she had tried her very best.

The glow of a woman in love!

The realisation caused his heart to pound unevenly in his chest, sending a flurry of panic through his veins. How could this have happened? How could he have been so blind? All he'd wanted was to possess her, have his fill of her, and then let her go on her way again.

He was in a danger zone here because, and he hated to admit this even to himself, he too was in that risky situation of feeling more for Elena than he had ever anticipated.

For tonight though he would push all such thoughts out of his mind. This was Elena's day. She had been so excited. It had never dawned on him in the beginning how selfish he was being. He'd wanted her body and little else. Now he was forced to admit that he had been seriously self-indulgent.

And it had backfired.

Splendidly.

After tonight he would need to take a serious look at himself and decide where his future lay.

Elena's parents weren't coming. Her mother didn't feel up to it and her father refused to leave her, but she had invited relatives and some friends from before she went to America. It was good to see her so alive and so happy.

He kissed her deeply and satisfyingly. 'If it wasn't so close to party time I'd take you to bed,' he growled. 'You taste delicious and you look more stunning than ever. Red suits you. You should wear it more often.'

'I dress to please,' she said softly.

With a further groan he pulled her even harder against him, feeling the thrust of her breasts against his chest; he even fancied he could feel her nipples, taut and exciting, trying to penetrate the thin cotton of his shirt, to tangle with his chest hairs—to drive him insane!

'Don't say things like that,' he growled, 'or there'll be no party, only our own private one. Very private.' He kissed her again, his tongue playing games with hers, his heart thudding against his ribcage. He slid his hands lower to cup and squeeze her fantastic bottom, luxuriating in the way she wriggled against him, and, finding the slit in her skirt, he slid his fingers inside the edge of her panties.

What a convenient dress this was. Personally he loved it, but he went cold at the thought of what her other male guests might think. And then he forgot about them when his searching fingers found the hot and wet core of her, so ready for him that it took every ounce of his not inconsiderable will power to pull his hand away. If he hadn't the dress would have gone, everything would have been forgotten except his need of her.

'Later,' he promised gruffly.

Every cell in his body was on high alert. He knew that he would never be able to take his eyes off her. All he could think about was ripping off the red dress and sinking himself into her welcoming heat.

'Would you fasten my necklace, please?'

Vidal suddenly realised that Elena had taken it out of the box and was holding it against her throat.

'Of course.' He took the ends, but his fingers shook so much that it was over a minute before he finally managed to clip the ends together. He was too aware of the warmth of her skin against his fingers, the drifting fragrance of her perfume. This was going to be a night never to be forgotten, he was certain of that.

The gold looked striking against her smooth skin and she was right, it was exactly what the dress needed. He kissed her again, gently this time, merely touching his lips to hers. 'Time to go, *mi amor*, if you want to be ready to meet your guests.'

Elena found herself being invited to dance by one man after another. Her feet hardly touched the ground and she saw Vidal watching her even while he was dancing with someone else.

But then it was his turn. 'I cannot keep away from you any longer,' he murmured, sliding his arms around her, nibbling her neck and her ear lobe. 'I am jealous of every man who comes near you.'

Where their bodies touched fire ignited. When his lips claimed hers she felt drunk with happiness. There was no doubt about it—she was in love with him. She did not even stop to think what the consequences would be. She was deliriously happy and wanted this moment to last for ever.

She had thought that nothing could make her happier until she caught sight of a latecomer. Someone she had not invited. The gatecrasher wore a black cocktail dress, her eyes made up so that they looked enormous, her lips a slash of red, her long black hair gracing her shoulders in seductive waves.

Elena pulled herself out of Vidal's arms and raced across the lawn, screaming her sister's name.

CHAPTER TEN

THE sisters hugged and wept. It was an emotional moment for Elena, knowing that Reina was safe and well. She glanced across at Vidal and saw him staring at them, a harsh frown creasing his brow as he started to walk towards them.

In an instant she led Reina into the house. They needed to talk without being disturbed.

'We've all been so worried about you,' she said. 'Where have you been? Why did you run away and tell no one?'

Reina pulled a wry face. 'I needed space. I've been staying with a friend in London.'

'I can't believe this. *Mamá*'s not well, you know. She's been in hospital. Did she tell you? Have you been to see them?'

'Of course,' answered Reina. 'And they told me about the party, that's why I'm here. But *Mamá* said nothing about being ill. What's wrong with her? She doesn't look poorly.'

Reina had the same shaped face as Elena, but there the resemblance ended. She was good-looking, but she wasn't beautiful, with brown eyes, a short nose and a wide mouth. Her hair was her crowning glory, long and thick and silky.

'She's been worried sick about the bank,' answered Elena quietly. 'And while she was in hospital they discovered a heart murmur. She needs to seriously look after herself. No more stress, the doctor said.'

'Oh, my goodness,' cried Reina, her hands going to her mouth. 'I wish I had known—I wouldn't have stayed away so long. I would never have done this to her. I'm home for good now, though, so I'll be able to look after her. But tell me why you've married Vidal. I couldn't believe it when *Mamá* told me. Have you both suddenly discovered that you're in love?'

'Love?' questioned Elena sharply. 'That's the last thing I'd ever feel for him.' It wasn't easy denying the feelings that had begun to creep up on her. But they were so new, so secretive that she didn't want to tell anyone about them, and most definitely not her beloved sister.

'Then why did you marry him?'

Elena raised her eyebrows. 'Do you need to ask? You ran away from him, don't forget. Someone had to step in and save the day. Didn't *Mamá* and *Papá* tell you?' She was beginning to feel a tiny bit confused by her sister's apparent ignorance of events.

'It's why they sent for me,' she went on before Reina could answer. 'I was their last hope. I'm not blaming you for walking out, I understand why you did it, but it took a lot of guts, I assure you, and I shall be glad when it's all over, but—'

'Stop! I can't believe what I am hearing,' cut in Reina, her dark eyes narrowed and fierce all of a sudden.

'You're telling me that Vidal refused to go ahead with the merger unless you married him?'

Elena nodded. 'Wasn't that what you were going to do?'

'Yes, but—'

'Didn't you care that our parents might have lost their livelihood?'

'But they wouldn't have done.'

Elena lifted her brows, giving her sister a piercing look. 'How can you say that? The bank was in big trouble. Have you any idea of the impassioned plea they made? I was going to refuse, yes, but then *Mamá* was taken ill with the stress of it all so I really had no choice.'

Reina's eyes flashed darkly and angrily. 'Vidal Marquez! I could kill that man.'

Elena frowned. 'I don't understand. What are you talking about?'

Her sister expelled her breath fiercely. 'He accepted the fact that I didn't want to commit to a loveless marriage. He appreciated my being honest. He said that he could understand it.' Reina sucked in another breath and let it go again just as angrily. 'And declared that he would go ahead with the merger regardless.'

Elena felt her head begin to spin. This couldn't be true. Vidal was a lot of things, but he surely wasn't capable of such deceit? He wouldn't have married her just because—because he wanted her body. Would he? She went hot all over at the very thought.

'My guess is that Vidal went back to the original idea so that he could get you into his bed,' concluded Reina bitterly. 'The man's a rat—he should be hanged.'

To have her fears confirmed sent an even deeper chill through Elena's veins. She felt herself trembling all over.

Immediately Reina wrapped her sister in her arms. 'I'm sorry. I never dreamt this would happen. I saw you two together earlier and you looked very—intimate, happy even. Are you sharing his bed?'

Elena nodded dismally.

'Are you in love with him?'

'No!' It was an instant denial. 'Haven't I said that? I hate him. I hate everything he stands for. He's a snake in man's clothing. He's slimy and sneaky and— I cannot believe he did this. Even our parents were kept in the dark. They had no idea that he was prepared to go through with the deal. It's why they sent for me.'

Another shudder racked her body. 'To think that I gave up running my company to be here, to help our parents—and all for nothing! Why the hell did you run away, Reina, without telling them? Why didn't you set them straight?'

She couldn't understand her sister. If Vidal had been okay with her reneging on their deal, why had she done a disappearing act? It didn't make sense. Admittedly Reina wouldn't have known the mess she'd left behind, she had thought it would all be hunky-dory, yet in reality it was anything but.

Reina pulled a pained face. 'I just assumed that Vidal would tell them. I never dreamt that he would go back on his word. Maybe he was going to, but they sent for you before he got round to it, and then he took a fancy to you. You've grown up, little sister, in a spectacular way.'

Discovering that the only reason Vidal had married

her was because he lusted after her body sent shock wave after shock wave through Elena's entire system. That, and the fact that she had given in to him so easily, so completely, even imagining that she was falling in love with him, made her feel physically sick. The very thought of what she had done, what *he* had done, what she had got herself into, sent her mind reeling into space.

Reina took Elena by the shoulders before speaking again. 'Look, Elena, maybe there is another explanation for all this. Surely Vidal wouldn't do such a thing. You looked happy before, dancing together, and he is gorgeous. You were within your rights to fall for him.'

Elena smiled at her sister, but it was filled with bitterness. Oh, Vidal might appear a gentleman, but Reina's revelation also put him into another category. A reprehensible deceiver. A man with no principles. So what was she to do about it? How could she carry on living with him knowing what he was like, what he had done? Vidal had touched every pulse in her body. He had made her his in every sense of the word.

'He has the morals of a gutter snake,' she snapped, fury stiffening her spine, causing her golden eyes to practically shoot sparks into the air. 'And I shall delight in telling him so.'

Vidal had charmed her into falling in love with him, but she had to discard those feelings now. He was not worthy of her love. He had tricked her in the worst way possible. How would she ever be able to trust him again?

Besides, he didn't have the same sort of feelings for her. He treated her well, he bought her expensive gifts, he was a fantastic lover, but behind it all was the hard businessman. He'd had an eye for a deal and she had been his stepping stone towards it.

All thoughts that he'd been warming towards her fled. He wouldn't hesitate to get rid of her when their contract ended—she knew that now. And he was going to be in for a very rude awakening if he thought she would stay the term. This was the end of the line as far as she was concerned.

Vidal wondered how much longer they were going to be. Reina turning up like this had been a worst-case scenario. He had been on the verge of confessing to Elena that he was falling in love with her. The very words had been on his lips. He had been going to suggest that they start afresh and turn their marriage into a real one.

And now Reina had put in an appearance, and if she had told her sister the true state of affairs she would have ruined everything!

He had never felt like this about any other woman. Elena made him feel totally different about himself. She had drawn out a side of him that he had never known existed. A softer side, a caring side. Instead of thinking only about his banking interests, he'd had this totally stunning woman to fill his mind.

She not only fulfilled his physical needs, but his mental ones as well. She was stimulating company, they had had conversations on all manner of subjects, making him want to spend every second of his time with her.

Yes, he had behaved despicably, but who could blame him? How else could he have got her into his bed? He was ashamed of that now, deeply ashamed. He had to talk to her, he had to convince her that he was genuinely sorry. There were other ways he could have gone about it. He could have pursued her without marrying her—even if he'd had to go to LA to do it. What had he been thinking?

Admittedly, good had come out of their arrangement—she had developed feelings for him too. He had seen it in her eyes, in the way her body responded. She gave herself to him freely and willingly now, sometimes even being the instigator. Surely she wouldn't behave like that unless she was falling in love with him too?

How much longer were they going to be? The waiting was driving him insane. They were pulling him to pieces, he knew that without a doubt. He could not wait any longer. It was time to intervene.

He found them upstairs in Elena's own private sitting room. When he pushed open the door two pairs of accusing eyes stared at him. The atmosphere was so thick he could have cut it with a knife.

Reina stood up, her back ramrod straight, flaring her brown eyes. 'You're the lowest of the low, Vidal Marquez. To think I once thought you were a man of integrity. How could you do this to my sister?'

Vidal drew in a short, sharp breath. How could he indeed? But this was between him and Elena, not Reina. 'I'd be grateful if you'd leave us alone,' he said, trying his hardest to keep his voice soft and even. It was difficult when he was facing what had to be the most crucial conversation of his life.

Reina turned her head. 'Do you want me to stay, Elena?'

Elena shook her head, her eyes devoid of all feeling. 'No. I'll deal with this.'

Reluctantly Reina left, giving Vidal another accusatory glare as she walked past him.

When they were alone, when the door had closed, Vidal moved slowly towards Elena, his eyes sad and full of self-reproach.

Contrastingly Elena's eyes sparked into life and she jumped to her feet. 'Don't even try to make excuses. In fact, I never want to see you again. I want you to go and tell our guests that the party is over. Or would you like me to do it? I could tell them a few home truths at the same time.'

Vidal felt an acute pain in the region of his heart. He had done this to her. He deserved her anger, but he could not walk away from this relationship without trying to repair the damage. 'Elena, you're hurt and distraught, I understand that, but—'

'You bet I'm hurt,' she cried. 'I've never felt so humiliated in my whole life. I never want to see you again, Vidal. I want nothing to do with you. First thing in the morning I'm out of here. Now go, get rid of all those people out there.'

Infierno, she looked beautiful, her eyes burning with passion, her cheeks flaming. She stood proud and tall, her red dress a symbol of her anger, of the rage that filled her with such fire. He desperately wanted to hold her in his arms, to kiss her better as one might a child. He wanted to say sorry over and over again.

But he could see that she was determined he leave, and although he would prefer to stay and sort things out between them, try to convince her that he wasn't all bad, that he would spend the rest of his life making it up to her, he knew that it would be wise to give her some time on her own.

Perhaps in a few hours she would feel differently. She would realise that although his motives hadn't been exactly altruistic, there was no denying that their feelings for each other were now very real.

Reluctantly he left the room, explaining to their guests that Elena wasn't feeling well. Nevertheless it was almost an hour before the last one left, before the caterers took away the food that no one had yet touched, before the band packed up their instruments.

Elena had changed out of her red dress into a pair of trousers and a T-shirt by the time Vidal found her again. She was furiously, furiously angry. He had caused her the ultimate humiliation. And she had fallen for it. That was the worst part. She had listened to his plans, seen no other way of helping her parents—and yet all the time he had wanted only her body.

She felt violated, stupid, embarrassed.

'What are you doing?' he asked, looking at her open suitcase.

'What does it look like I'm doing?' she retorted, turning around to glare at him. 'I'm moving out.' There was no way on this earth that she could sleep with him, stay with him, pretend with him. Not any more. It was over, finished. She never wanted to see him again as long as she lived.

'I won't let you do that. We can sort this out. We need to talk. I want to explain.'

Vidal closed the gap between them, standing so close that she could smell the cologne he had splashed on earlier. It had always kicked her hormones into life, it was as much an intrinsic part of Vidal as any physical element of him. But tonight it did nothing. She felt as though she were made of stone. She had no heart, she had no feelings—nothing except anger.

'What is there to explain?' she demanded, her golden eyes flaring magnificently. 'You forced me to marry you because you wanted my body. Have you any idea how humiliating that is? I feel sick every time I think about it. I—'

'Elena, will you please listen?'

He attempted to take her into his arms, but she stepped back. 'To what? Another pack of lies? You disgust me, Vidal.'

'Maybe I did desire you,' he admittedly quietly. 'You're too utterly gorgeous for any man not to like what he sees. But that wasn't the only reason I—'

'Save the excuses,' she spat. 'I know what sort of a man you are. A scheming, manipulative, devious bastard. I hate you. I never want to see you again as long as I live.' She turned her back on him, her shoulders hunched, not wanting him to see the tears in her eyes.

It could have all been so beautiful. Tonight she really had thought that she was in love with him. He had made her feel special and it had promised to be a birthday to surpass all birthdays. It had done that all right! This was a birthday she would never forget. Not as long as she lived.

She felt his hands on her shoulders, gentle, tentative, and they sent waves of anguish through her body. 'Don't touch me,' she cried. 'Get away from me.' And she swung round to meet the sad silver of his eyes.

'We need to talk,' he said quietly, 'properly talk, but we can't do so until you've calmed down.'

'You think I'll ever recover from this?' Elena found it hard to believe that he was still trying to talk her round. 'No words will ever put the matter right. What is done is done. It cannot be undone. I'll never forgive you. Not in a million years.'

And it wasn't only the fact that he had hurt and humiliated her, he had deceived her parents as well. How were they going to feel when they found out?

They mustn't. She must never tell them, it would break their hearts, it would send her mother into hospital again—and this time she might not recover. Oh, God, how had she let herself get into this mess? Vidal was a monster. Thinking only of himself, his own pleasure, his own needs.

Every time she thought about the way she had given her body to him, willingly at times, lovingly even, she wanted to stab a knife into his heart.

'Perhaps in the morning you might think differently. My motives were entirely—'

'Dishonourable!' Elena's eyes met his head-on. 'Don't think you can talk your way out of this, Vidal.' Her whole body was on fire; she wanted to flail her fists against his chest; she wanted to hurt him as he had hurt her. Except that no amount of physical violence would ever heal the hurt in her heart. It was doubtful it would ever go away. She had been a stupid, silly fool, taken in by a handsome face and carefully spoken words.

'I think you should get some sleep,' he said quietly. 'Perhaps you'll feel better in the morning. We can talk then.'

She strode across to the door. 'Perhaps *you* will sleep. Perhaps your conscience won't affect you. If you have one, that is. I'll use another room tonight, Vidal, and then tomorrow I'll be gone. Out of your life. For ever.'

She slammed the door behind her, half expecting it to be pulled open again, for him to follow, not knowing whether to be relieved or surprised when he didn't. Both perhaps. She was most definitely surprised; she had expected him to stop her, to come after her, to make a further attempt to excuse his behaviour.

Except that there were no excuses. What he had done was unpardonable.

And her relief that he was giving her time to herself, that he wasn't coming after her and forcing her to continue the conversation when she felt like drowning her sorrows in a bottle of something strong and intoxicating, knew no bounds. There was nothing else left for them to say. He had hurt her immeasurably, she felt used and defiled, and it would be a long, long time before she ever trusted another man. If ever!

She pushed open one of the other bedroom doors and curled up on the bed fully dressed. She wouldn't sleep— how could she when her mind was in turmoil? Tears spilled down her cheeks as she lay there sobbing silently. Never had she met a man whom she hated as much as she hated Vidal now.

If her sister hadn't turned up she would have given her heart to him. Thank goodness she hadn't. Because once given she wouldn't have been able to take it back. Once she had confessed her love he would never have let her go. It would have bound her to him as surely as if she were held in shackles.

Never in her wildest imaginings had she dreamt that Vidal would be capable of such duplicity. He had worked his magic on her, and she had fallen for it hook, line and sinker.

The first pale fingers of dawn were spreading across the sky when she finally fell asleep. A deeply troubled sleep where her dreams were peppered with visions of Vidal. Sometimes he had the horns of a devil and was mocking her. At others his face was gentle, his eyes filled with love, and she would reach out her arms, only for him to fade away before she could touch him.

Unaware that she was crying out in her sleep, thrashing her arms and tossing her head from side to side, Elena opened her eyes to find Vidal bending over her, trying to still her frenzied movements, touching a gentle hand to her brow.

'You were dreaming,' he said quietly.

Elena knocked his arm away. 'I was having a nightmare. And it was about you.' He even had the nerve to look as though he cared. How could he? Damn the man! She swung away from him, rolling to the other side of the bed and standing up.

'Elena—'

They stood within inches of each other now, eyeball to eyeball. Neither moving a muscle. The only sound in the room was her own heart beating. Thud! Thud! Thud! Loud enough to echo in her ears and make her feel faint. Which was ridiculous. She had to be strong, she needed to be strong. This man had tricked her big time.

'We need to talk.'

'There is nothing left to say. Nothing that will make any difference.'

'I think there is. You need to listen to my side of—'

'Vidal, am I not making myself clear? I do not want this conversation.'

'I am sorry I deceived you,' he said quietly, his eyes shadowed and full of pain.

'It's not good enough,' she answered.

'More sorry than you'll ever know. It was a stupid idea. I should have known that Reina would return one day and you'd learn the truth.'

'But surprisingly it never occurred to you.' Elena's voice was filled with derision. 'I don't know who's the most stupid, you or me.'

'I don't want you to go.'

'Try stopping me!'

'The least we need to do, Elena, is sit down and discuss the matter.' His eyes pleaded with her to listen. 'I've made a terrible mistake, I'm fully aware of that, but there has to be some way out of it. I'm—I've grown very fond of you. You've become a part of my life, you've added to it, you've—'

Elena's eyes flashed. 'Spare me the sob story.'

'Unfortunately I have to go to the office this morning. Something's cropped up that needs my personal attention. Promise me you'll be here when I get back.'

'Not if there's a flight home, I won't,' she claimed, locking her eyes into his, seeing his misery, but he couldn't be hurting as much as she was. She felt as raw as if she had been whipped.

'I need a shower,' she said bluntly.

'Then I'll see you later. Don't run out on me, Elena.'

The warning note in his voice did not escape her. But it made no difference. She was still going to leave.

Except that when she telephoned the airline she discovered that there were no direct flights to LA today. She could of course go home to her parents, but then her mother would worry and that was the last thing she wanted. With a bit of luck Reina had not said anything yet about the state of affairs.

She would speak to them in her own good time, and hopefully make them believe that Vidal had released her from their marriage early.

After booking a flight for the next day Elena impulsively decided to take Jet out. She needed escapism and Jet was such an amazing horse that she felt as though she were flying when she was on his back. Riding him would clear her head and make her strong enough to face Vidal and insist that enough was enough.

His head stable hand had other ideas though. 'I've had my instructions, Señora Marquez. You are not to take Jet out again. If you do I will lose my job.'

Elena had known he would say this, but she was determined to have her own way. It was amazing what a few softly spoken words and a winning smile achieved. She assured him that he would not lose his job, that she would put matters right with his master.

Following the same path beside the river that she had taken before, Elena once again gave Jet his rein. In no time at all she began to feel better. He was such a magnificent beast, she could understand why Vidal would never let anyone else ride him. He was powerful and strong like his owner. And she couldn't help wondering whether in the horse world Jet was the master, bending all the other horses to his will.

Before long they left the river and headed up into the hills, Jet picking his sure-footed way, sometimes carefully, at others racing as though all the hounds in hell were on his tail. It was the most exhilarating feeling in the world and she was able to forget her anger and distress, laughing out loud, relishing the feel of this strong beast beneath her.

Until—suddenly and unexpectedly—Jet stumbled. He went down on his forelegs and Elena pitched forward over his head. There was nothing she could do to stop herself.

It seemed like for ever that she rolled down the hillside, her body bouncing against the hard earth, crushing branches, bruising her limbs, before coming to an abrupt halt as she slammed into an oak tree. After that she knew no more.

On his way home Vidal ran over in his mind the conversation he intended having with Elena. He intended to beg her forgiveness, promise her anything, the world, if she would only stay. He had been foolish to believe he could get away with the pretence that her parents would lose their bank. It had been childish and manipulative and he found it hard to believe now that he had actually thought it would work.

To his dismay there was no sign of Elena. He took the stairs two at a time, his heart sinking as low as it could get at the thought that she had already left. But her suitcase was still there. Packed and locked, no clothes left in her dressing room, so she *was* going— but where was she now?

He searched the grounds, checked the swimming

pool, the stables. He could not believe what he was hearing when he was told that she had taken Jet out.

'Didn't I leave express instructions that she was never to ride him again?' he roared, feeling his heart bang uneasily against his ribcage.

'Your wife, she is a very determined lady, señor,' said his stable hand. 'I am sorry, it was impossible to stop her.'

'Impossible!' snorted Vidal. 'What sort of talk is that? Never mind, don't answer, I know what she is like.' As stubborn as a mule. He had hurt her unbearably, but for her to take out Jet again, in the mood she was in—the consequences didn't bear thinking about.

'Saddle me up one of the other horses,' he instructed. He had no intention of standing around waiting for her return. This was all his fault. He felt as guilty as hell now, and if anything had happened to her…

But then, as before, he heard the clip clop of hooves. He swung round, words of relief on his lips, but his thoughts stopped right there when he saw that Jet was riderless. His heart came into his mouth. Unless she was following on foot? Maybe Jet had thrown her and she was limping along feeling slightly foolish.

But there was no sign of Elena. Just the horse. Returned home like the faithful friend he was. He even had a faintly hangdog expression as though he knew that he had done wrong. The question now was where was Elena? Was she lying hurt somewhere? Maybe she was even lost. Which route had they taken? She could be anywhere. The area around them was endless. There were woods and scrubby areas and the river.

The river! What if she'd got thrown into the river and

drowned? Or what if she was unconscious somewhere up in the mountain, somewhere inaccessible where no one would ever find her? He had only himself to blame. Everything was his fault. Why the hell had he thought he would ever get away with it?

The horse came to nuzzle him and Vidal patted his nose. 'You're coming with me, boy. We have to find her.'

He sprang into the saddle and even though the stirrups were too short he didn't want to waste time lengthening them. He urged Jet into a gallop as they covered the ground he imagined they might have taken, and the longer he was out there, the more concerned and distressed he became.

They left the river and climbed the mountain, his horse seeming to know exactly where to go. But after a while the animal grew tired, and Vidal was nearing his wit's end—when he thought he heard a sound. He brought Jet to a halt and they stood still and silent. There it was again. A faint, 'Help!'

'Elena!' he shouted. 'I'm coming. Where are you?'

He followed the sound of her voice, his heart beating a million times a minute when he saw her lying motionless. Every vestige of colour was drained from her face and one leg was pinned beneath a log.

Immediately he was down on his knees beside her. 'Elena, you scared me to death. When Jet came home on his own I immediately thought the worst. I thank my lucky stars that you are alive. Are you in pain?'

'My leg…' she said faintly.

'I'm going to lift the log off you. Tell me if it hurts too much.'

He watched her face just in case her leg might be

broken. But she didn't flinch, she simply lay there pale and lifeless.

'Never, ever do this to me again, Elena.'

She didn't answer. Why would she when she was hell-bent on leaving him?

'Can you move your leg?'

She tried warily and nodded.

'Are you hurt anywhere else?'

'I don't think so.'

'Nevertheless you're going to hospital to be checked out.'

'Whatever you say, Vidal,' she whispered, and then fainted.

CHAPTER ELEVEN

VIDAL cursed. He should have brought someone with him. It had been a crazy idea coming to look for Elena alone. He couldn't leave her now and yet he needed help. He checked his cell phone. No signal, of course. Was there ever when you really needed it? *Infierno!* What now?

'Elena,' he said, stroking the soft skin of her cheek. 'Elena, can you hear me?'

Gradually she stirred, opening her eyes again and looking straight into his. *Dios!* All he wanted to do was hold her close and kiss her better. He had only himself to blame that she had taken Jet out again. He had let her down big-time.

What sort of a fool would insist on a temporary marriage for no other reason than he wanted her in his bed? With the added danger that her sister might return and tell her the truth? He had to have been seriously insane to believe that he would get away with it.

When he had seen her at that dinner, though, when he had decided there and then that he wanted her, he hadn't given Reina a thought. He'd put his own selfish needs first. And now look what had happened. Never in his life had he felt so foolish.

'I'm going to lift you up, Elena,' he said gently. 'Put your arms around my neck, but tell me if it hurts too much. It's the only way I'm going to get you out of here.'

Slowly she did so, and with strength born of desperation Vidal managed to lift her onto the horse. He sat behind and with his arms securely around her they walked sedately back to the house where he phoned for an ambulance.

Elena kept drifting in and out of consciousness and he was desperately worried. She hadn't worn a hat so could have banged her head and be suffering from concussion as well as an injured leg. Where the hell were they? Why was it taking so long?

It was actually only a few minutes before the medics arrived even though it felt like hours. Vidal accompanied Elena in the ambulance, murmuring words of comfort, though he was not sure that she could hear them. She had drifted again into her own world where there was no pain, either mental or physical.

Of one thing he was sure now: he loved this woman more than life itself. Deeply and truly and irrevocably. He couldn't imagine life without Elena. If anything serious had happened to her then his own life wouldn't be worth living.

It had been naïve of him to believe that he could use her and then discard her. How stupid and insensitive was that? Elena was not the sort of woman to let herself be used. She had come to him in all good faith, doing what she believed was right, and he had let her down. No wonder she'd been angry when her sister had told her the truth, no wonder she'd wanted to leave him. Not only had he let her down, but he had let himself down as well.

'I'm sorry, Elena,' he whispered, unsure whether she could hear him but feeling that he needed to say it. 'I was wrong, I was foolish, will you ever forgive me?'

At the hospital she was hurried away and all Vidal could do was pace and wait. It felt like an eternity before anyone came to see him, an eternity while he imagined the worst. Brain damage perhaps? She would never be the same again. And it was entirely his fault. She wouldn't be in this position if he hadn't forced her to marry him.

He had taken her away from a job she loved in LA, from her own business for pity's sake. What sort of a monster was he? So sure of himself. So cockily self-sure that he had taken her without any thought what he might be doing to her.

His head was bent low in his hands when the doctor approached. 'Señor Marquez?'

'*Sí.*' Vidal jumped swiftly to his feet. 'How is my wife? Can I see her?'

For the first time it felt different, saying 'my wife'. Before, it had been no more than a general term. But now, knowing that he loved her, it felt more personal. It felt good, actually. He was her husband, she was his wife. They were a couple, a *real* married couple.

Except that Elena did not love him. Elena wanted to leave him. He hadn't thought this far before, too amazed by his own discovery and the importance of it. But now it struck him that Elena did not return his feelings. She had made the best of a bad job, but was now determined to return home.

He had ruined everything by his own selfish greed.

'In all good time,' answered the doctor. 'First things first.'

First things first! What did that mean? It sounded ominous. As though he was preparing him for something unpleasant. 'What is wrong?' he asked swiftly and urgently, his brow dark now, a frown slashing across it. 'Tell me.'

'Nothing at all is wrong,' answered the man, smiling now. 'We've given your wife a thorough examination. She will be sore and bruised for a few days, but fortunately there are no major injuries. She's very lucky.'

'So can I see her now?' he asked, breathing more easily.

'And even luckier still that she didn't lose her baby.'

Vidal froze.

His heart stopped beating. The world stopped moving. The whole room faded away until there was nothing left except the doctor's positive face, a pair of brown eyes smiling into his. A baby? Elena was pregnant with his child and she hadn't told him! Mixed emotions flared through his mind. 'Are you sure?'

Mistaking his question for concern about his unborn child the doctor smiled. 'We've carried out a scan. All is well. Baby's heartbeat is just as it should be. You can go to her now. She's still shaken, but there does not appear to be any serious damage. Nevertheless we'll keep her in overnight to make certain, and when she gets home you must ensure that she gets plenty of rest for a few days for the baby's sake. Although they're resilient little creatures, this one has had a big shaking up.'

A fresh wave of feelings rippled through Vidal—it was the strangest feeling in the world, an incredibly emotional one! He had created another being. Perhaps someone in his own image, with a little bit of Elena thrown in.

His heart had started beating again, rattling along at a terrific rate, as it did when he made love. And he didn't dare speak for fear that he gave away the fact that he hadn't even known his wife was pregnant. What sort of impression would that give? But he was so full of emotion that his chest felt as though it wanted to burst wide open.

He was irked that Elena hadn't told him, but also oddly buoyant. If the Reina affair hadn't blown up there would have come a time when the evidence would be irrefutable and she'd have had to say something. Perhaps she'd been afraid? Afraid of his reaction. Afraid he might have accused her of trapping him.

Or perhaps she had never planned to tell him at all. Perhaps she'd intended returning to LA in any case. It had just brought things forward when her sister put in her appearance. His lips thinned at the thought of her leaving. Over his dead body!

The doctor's words cut into his thoughts. 'Come, Señor Marquez, I will take you to your wife.'

Although Elena had her eyes closed she knew the exact moment when Vidal entered the room, and she was afraid to look at him after what the doctor had told her.

She was carrying Vidal's baby!

It was her worst nightmare come true.

Elena knew exactly when it had happened—in the shower by the pool, the first time he had taken her, when they had both been too caught up in their own screamingly intense feelings to even think about contraception. Since then he had always, but always, taken precautions.

Even her missed period hadn't worried her because she'd put it down to the emotional trauma she was going through. Now, though, she was facing the biggest dilemma of her life.

A temporary marriage had been bad enough, but to be bound to Vidal for ever because she had stupidly allowed herself to get pregnant. How ridiculous was that! And the fact that she had unwittingly fallen in love with him made it ten times worse. Nevertheless he had deceived her big-time and she would never forgive him, not ever.

'Elena?' Vidal bent low over her bed, one hand either side of her, his face close to hers. She had no choice but to look at him.

There was tenderness and concern in his eyes, his voice so soft as to be almost inaudible. 'Are you all right, *mi querida*?'

She gave the faintest of nods, not daring to speak in case she gave away her fear.

There was nothing in his expression to suggest that he knew about the baby. Perhaps the doctor hadn't said anything, leaving it to her to tell her husband that the tiny scrap of humanity inside her was safe and well. As if she would! As soon as she felt up to it she was flying back to LA. She would bring this child up on her own. Vidal could go to hell.

He bent his head lower and touched his lips to hers. 'I've been out of my mind with worry. You took a bad fall, Elena. You're very lucky to have no serious injuries.'

'I know. Thank you for finding me. I'm not sure I could have made it home.' Thanking him was the least she could do.

'I'm damn sure you couldn't have done. You were out of it for most of the time.' His voice rose, became gruff, and then softened again almost immediately. 'The doctor wants to keep you in overnight, just to make sure there are no after-effects. And he wants you to rest now, so I must leave. I'll be back in the morning.'

He touched his lips to hers, looked at her long and hard, and then walked quietly away.

When he had gone Elena closed her eyes again, breathing out, relaxing her limbs, unaware of how tense she had grown these last few minutes. The discovery that she was carrying Vidal's baby was proving too much to take in.

She felt drowsy again now and sleep claimed her. Perfect, dreamless sleep. When she awoke the first thing she thought about was her baby. She put a hand to her stomach again, finding it hard to believe that there was a new life growing. The very thought made her smile briefly.

It was not how she'd planned her time with Vidal to end and, although she desperately wanted to say nothing, to disappear out of his life and bring the baby up herself, there were also her parents to consider. Without a doubt they would spread the news. Their first grandchild! He would find out one way or another.

But it still didn't mean that she had to stay with him.

After breakfast the doctor came to see her and shortly after that Vidal arrived. His smile was warm and concerned, making Elena feel a little guilty at the thought of keeping her condition from him. Not that he deserved to know—he didn't deserve anything. She would hate him to the end of her days for tricking her into this marriage.

'How are you feeling?' he asked quietly.

'A little bruised, a little sore, but otherwise okay,' she answered. 'I'm free to go home so long as I rest.'

Vidal's smile widened. 'I've brought you some clean clothes.'

'Thank you.' His thoughtfulness did not surprise her. But the fact that he had been going through her drawers to find clean undies made her skin go warm. The idea of this big man's hands touching her delicate briefs, deciding which bra she should wear, did they need to match, did colour matter, caused all sorts of feelings to race through her body.

Elena slid off the bed, took the case and disappeared into the bathroom. Vidal had chosen a pair of loose-fitting cotton trousers and a T-shirt, both in shades of pale pink. She guessed that he had decided on something soft because of her bruising and she reluctantly appreciated it because she was most definitely very tender in places.

She really had been foolish taking Jet out again. And even more foolish allowing the horse his head on such difficult terrain. It could have all ended so differently. She could have broken her leg; she could even have been killed.

For one very brief moment she thought that even that might have been better than bringing Vidal's baby into the world. But then she dismissed it. The baby hadn't asked for any of this. He was the innocent pawn in the game they had played. He deserved the very best in life and she was determined to give it him. Without Vidal's help!

In the limousine on their way home he constantly asked whether she was all right until in the end Elena snapped, 'For pity's sake, Vidal, stop fussing. I had a fall, that's all. I'm not made of glass. I didn't break. Just leave me alone.'

His mouth tightened and he threw her a pained glance that suggested she was hurting his feelings, but she didn't care. He hadn't thought of her feelings when he'd demanded that she marry him.

Once they were home Vidal insisted on her sitting comfortably in the garden room, constantly asking whether there was anything she needed. Elena felt like screaming. She would have preferred his anger, it would have helped in her decision to leave. Instead she had to put up with his undivided attention.

It unsettled her.

'Shouldn't you be at work?' she enquired, when he asked for what seemed like the hundredth time whether she wanted anything.

'And leave you in this condition?' he promptly returned, his silver eyes gentle on her face.

'What condition? I'm bruised, yes, and sore, my leg hurts, but I'm not ill. I fell, that's all. There's enough staff here to look after me.' For pity's sake, she wasn't an invalid.

'You're also pregnant!'

Elena stopped breathing. Everything inside her clenched. Her senses went on high alert. She chanced a look into Vidal's face, seeing recrimination now, seeing a toughness that had been noticeably absent.

'The doctor told you?' It was a stupid question because how else could he have known? But what was she supposed to say when she hadn't even known herself?

'What I'm wondering is why you didn't tell me?'

She heard controlled anger and shuddered. She was still feeling a little delicate if the truth were known and could do without the third degree.

'I'm wondering if you ever would have told me, or whether your decision to leave had something to do with it?'

'There is a simple explanation.' Elena heard the defence in her voice and wished she had been able to speak normally. She didn't feel up to confrontation. Why couldn't he have waited a few days until she was back to normal, strong enough to stick up for herself?

'There is?' Dark, masculine brows rose imperiously.

'I didn't know myself.' She managed to say the words coolly and calmly, her eyes not moving from his. 'Do you think I would have rode Jet the way I did if I'd known? Credit me with some sense, Vidal.'

'You didn't wonder?'

The crisp sharpness in his voice sent a shiver down her spine. 'I didn't even think about it.' Her eyes challenged his, gold against silver, heat against heat.

'Do I take it that you actually mean that? That you really didn't know?'

'I'm not a liar.'

Some of the wind went out of his sails. She saw his shoulders relax, the hard lines on his face soften. But his eyes were still narrowed. 'What would you have done when the truth eventually hit you? Would you have told me then?'

'As I was already planning to leave, no, I can't answer that,' she returned, keeping her voice silken smooth and her chin high.

The scowl was back, anger darkening his eyes to a stormy grey, and Elena realised that she shouldn't have said that. Forewarning him was dangerous.

'And you really think I would have allowed you to leave?'

'I guess you'd have tried to stop me.'

'You're damn well right,' he snarled. 'I *would* have stopped you. This baby's not your sole responsibility. I am the baby's father, for God's sake,' he added on a roar. 'And no one, not even you, will deny me my parental rights.'

'Parental rights be damned,' she flung back, equally angry now. 'You want this baby no more than I do. But what is done is done. I will be the best mother to him in the world. He won't need a father.'

'*Dios!*' Vidal exploded. 'I—'

'And I don't really think you should be upsetting me in the condition I am in,' she tagged on for good measure.

It stopped Vidal dead in his tracks. For a moment he simply stood and stared at her, then his voice softened, his eyes lost some of their hardness. 'We need to talk about this.'

'What is there to say?' She did not want to commit

to him for ever. When she had agreed to a temporary marriage she had done so in all good faith. Never dreaming that he was tricking her, never dreaming that this would happen. That her life would change irrevocably.

All of a sudden her head began to spin. She saw Vidal start towards her, but she knew no more until she opened her eyes and found that she was lying on their bed—the bed she had shared with Vidal!

He was looking down at her with a worried expression in his eyes. 'What happened?' she asked huskily.

'You passed out. I think the doctor ought to see you again. Maybe they shouldn't have let you out until—'

'I'm fine,' insisted Elena.

'I shouldn't have got cross with you.' Vidal took her hand and held it firmly between both of his. 'I should have let things pass until you were feeling stronger. We'll say no more on the matter.'

For now, she thought bitterly. But it wouldn't be long before he started insisting again that her place was with him—permanently! The thought filled her with dread. This was a man who had had no compunction about making her his wife for his own personal reasons. What would happen when he tired of her?

Would he tire of their child too? Her head ached. There was so much to think about. 'I'd like to rest for a little while,' she said quietly, thankful when Vidal took the hint and reluctantly left the room.

At the door he turned and looked back at her, but he didn't say anything. There was surprising sadness in his eyes, which mystified her slightly. What did he have to be sad about? Anger she could understand. Rage and frustration. But sadness?

Vidal felt as though his heart were breaking. For the first time in his adult life he felt close to tears. Elena was the most amazing woman he had ever met and he didn't want her to leave. Life would be unbearable without her. One way or another he needed to persuade her to stay.

It was not going to be easy. He had treated her unfairly and had a lot of making up to do. But maybe the fact that she was carrying his baby in her womb would help. The main thing was to keep a hold on his temper, treat her with kid gloves; not give her any further reason to feel she had to leave.

The thought that she was pregnant with his child caused odd sensations. He imagined himself for the very first time in his life as a father. Holding a tiny new-born baby in his arms, watching him grow—he hoped it was a boy. Playing with him, teaching him, advising him. Taking care of his education, seeing him into adulthood. Standing proud when he got married. And one day his son would become a father too. He would be given the same heart-stopping information that he himself had been given yesterday.

And he wanted to be there for him. He didn't believe in single mothers, and he most certainly didn't want some other man bringing up his son as his own. Oh, no. He would use all of his persuasive powers to make Elena stay.

What it would take he didn't know. It would be a case of feeling his way. She naturally had her business to consider. Would she give it up? Would she sell it? Bringing up a child would take all of her time and energy. He didn't want his wife working when there was no need.

All of these thoughts went through his head as he

waited for Elena to awake. He could have gone to work but he knew that he would be unable to concentrate. He wanted to sort things out with her once and for all. Only then would he settle back into his routine.

Creeping upstairs, he sat on a chair and watched her. Her cheeks were faintly flushed, her breathing even, and she looked incredibly beautiful. He wanted to burrow into the bed at her side, be there when she awoke, when those fantastic golden eyes looked into his.

He didn't dare, though. For once in his life he was afraid. Afraid of losing the one woman he had ever truly fallen in love with.

CHAPTER TWELVE

WHEN Elena awoke the first thing she saw was Vidal sitting in a chair at the side of the bed, a faint frown creasing the space between his eyes as he looked at her. She had forgotten in that first instant about their argument, or even that she was pregnant with his child. She had felt relaxed and refreshed but now memories came tumbling back.

It was the biggest wonder in the world that the baby had not been hurt when she fell. She stretched her limbs experimentally and groaned. Everything still ached and hurt. Was baby hurting too?

'How long have I been asleep?' she asked him quietly.

Vidal's smile was gentle. 'A couple of hours, I guess.'

'And you've sat here all that time?' It disturbed her to discover that he had been watching her as she slept. It was an intrusion of privacy. She was still fully dressed, but that made no difference. It was the fact that Vidal had watched every breath she drew, every movement she made. It was the biggest wonder in the world that he hadn't climbed onto the bed beside her and held her in his arms.

He hadn't wanted her to leave when she found out about his deception, but now that she was pregnant he would be even more possessive. It was going to be even harder to get away from him.

'I feel responsible,' he said softly. 'It is my fault that you're hurt.'

Elena frowned. 'How can it be your fault?'

'I deceived you.'

'I can't argue with that.' He had deceived her big-time and it was no good him looking contrite now because it made no difference. She was still leaving as soon as she felt up to it. She would move in with her parents temporarily before going back to LA. Whether she stayed there or came back remained to be seen. Of only one thing was she sure: she didn't want Vidal to be a part of her life any longer.

It would be hard, as she knew he would insist on them staying together for their baby's sake. It wouldn't work, though. She would never be able to forget what he had done. She would need to be strong.

'I want to make it up to you.'

With a flash of her beautiful eyes Elena pushed herself up, swinging her legs over the side of the bed so that she sat facing him. 'How long do you have—for ever? Because I shall never forgive you.'

Vidal clamped his lips grimly together and looked at her long and hard. 'Never is a long time, Elena.'

There was a long moment's silence during which Vidal got to his feet, his eyes not leaving hers. They had gone stone-cold by this time, solid sheets of silver that threatened to slice right through her. And his next words were delivered with cutting precision. 'Do you really think I'd let you go? Our child needs both of his parents.'

Elena clenched her fists, her nails digging into her palms, but she felt no pain. She foresaw a battle ahead and she really didn't have the strength at this moment to fight Vidal. 'Would you mind leaving, Vidal?'

'Why? Because you don't want to face the fact that I am the child's father?' Vidal's powerful hands clenched her shoulders in a tight grip. 'Listen to me, Elena, we have a lot going for us, and especially now with the baby. You can't leave, Elena.'

His hard voice shuddered through her bones, making her realise what a tough opponent he was. Vidal in this mood was daunting and made her realise how tempting it would be to give in to him, to be with him again as they were before. Maybe they could make things work. Nevertheless she looked at him coldly. 'You won't be able to stop me.'

He stared at her long and hard, his eyes drilling through her, and she expected more harsh words, but instead he shocked her by abruptly turning on his heel and leaving the room.

Elena guessed that he had deemed it wise to go before he did or said something he regretted. She had never seen him quite like this before. The way he had come after her in the first place was nothing compared to the power he was trying to wield over her now.

She sat down on the edge of the bed, feeling shaky. She had meant every word. Vidal *had* used her; he had treated her with no respect. He had claimed her as his woman and she felt defiled, but still the shoots of her love for him lodged in her heart. It wasn't going to be easy getting away, but harder still to forget about the man, especially now she carried his most precious child.

Vidal stayed at home for the rest of the day, spending the afternoon in a video conference, but as soon as he was finished he devoted his time to her. Slowly and cleverly he wore down her defences with gentle attentiveness, pandering to her every need, almost foreguessing her wishes. He read to her and they talked about the news, never once touching upon the painful subject of the baby and Elena's leaving.

It was no surprise to Elena then that when Vidal gently kissed her goodnight it awoke the passion between them and somehow she ended up in his bed that night.

From her initially wanting to shut him out of her life, from her wanting nothing more to do with him *ever*, he had subtly despatched all her harsh thoughts. She had melted in his arms as though nothing untoward had ever happened between them.

She put it down to her condition. It had made her soft. Or was it that the love she had begun to feel for Vidal had never really gone away? It had been hidden beneath her anger and under his constant pressure, his alien gentleness, it had flowered again and taken her once more into a world where nothing mattered except fulfilment.

He was on one elbow now looking into her face and if Elena hadn't known better she would have sworn she could see love there. A glow shone in his eyes that was different from anything she had seen before. Something soft and warm, not normally associated with Vidal.

There was usually a hard glitter when he wanted to make love, a deep hungry need that had to be fulfilled.

And she had always been hungry enough to give him what he wanted, to let their bodies rise on a passionate storm of fearless sensations.

This was a new Vidal. One who stirred previously unknown feelings, who sent a warmth trickling slowly through her body until it encompassed her. He made her feel hungry for him and yet languid at the same time.

She closed her eyes and seconds later felt him trail kisses across the flat plane of her stomach, abrading her skin with his tongue, letting her know in so many different ways that he loved and worshipped her. Truly loved, not simply for the sake of the tiny baby they had created—who might even be aware of his father's caress.

And how did she know all this? she asked herself. How did she know it wasn't a concerted effort on his part to make her stay with him?

Because love recognised love.

Vidal was different now—everything he did came from his heart. The fact that he was about to become a father had possibly jolted him into seeing the truth. Here was a man who had always denied himself the joy of falling in love. He had found pleasure in women but he had wanted no commitment. But now he had found it and was prepared to—to what?

Elena jolted herself back to reality. Vidal had not spoken. She had come to this conclusion without him saying a word. What if she was mistaken? What if he truly was playing a game? What if she had misread the signals and all he wanted was his baby? How would she ever know?

'What is wrong?' Vidal lifted his head, his silver eyes

shadowed as he looked at her. 'Do you have a pain? Have I hurt you? Is there—?'

Elena shook her head. 'Nothing like that. But I need to ask you a question.' It was make or break time. She had to know one way or the other. 'And I want you to be perfectly honest.'

'In future I will never be anything less,' he assured her solemnly, sitting up straight and looking down at her anxious face.

Elena sat up too, her eyes resting on his. He had such beautiful eyes, they were almost her undoing. Instead of talking she wanted his kisses again; she wanted to feel him against her and inside her. She wanted to experience the unique passion they shared. In the aftermath of lovemaking it would be so much easier to ask him her question.

But it had to be done now, before an eruption of her senses blinded her vision. 'Do you love me, Vidal?'

There, she had said it! She felt colour flood her cheeks and the pinprick of a blush all over her body. She screwed up her face, wishing she could take the words back. How could she have asked him so bluntly? What would he think of her?

She held her breath.

His brows rose and for a few heart-stopping seconds she thought that he was not going to answer. But then he smiled, one of his smiles that made her feel good all over, that sent tremors through her veins and caused her pulses to quicken.

'How could I not be in love with an angel?'

Was she hearing him correctly? He had actually called her an angel! After the way she had raged at him?

'For that is what you are, my dearest, Elena. The kindest, most beautiful person I have ever known. You put your whole life on hold for the sake of your parents. You married a man you hardly knew, a man you pro-fessed to dislike, a man who deceived you disgracefully and will be eternally sorry for what he did. You are the most selfless woman I have ever known. I am surprised you need to ask the question.'

Elena felt her cheeks grow warm. This was more than she had expected and speech became impossible.

'Do you still have doubts?' His eyes didn't leave her face, gentle and unthreatening as he waited patiently for her answer. 'Or do you think my declaration of love is because of this?' He put his hand on her stomach and Elena instinctively put her own over it.

'It's something I need to be sure of,' she confessed quietly.

'Then let me put your mind at rest,' he cut in gently. 'I love you, *mi querida*. More than you will ever know. I confess I insisted on us getting married for selfish reasons. When I saw you at that charity dinner I wanted you badly. No other woman had ever managed to make me feel like you did. But I realise now that it wasn't purely your body I was after. I had fallen insanely and instantly in love.' His tone changed, became even softer. 'And you, my darling, do you think you will ever find it in your heart to forgive me, to fall in love with me too?'

Elena shivered. She wanted to avoid his eyes, but couldn't. They attracted her like a magnet. Like two beautiful silver magnets with dark, dark centres, intent on hers, waiting patiently for her answer.

'I am in love with you,' she whispered, hating the way another blush spread across her skin. 'That's why I was so hurt when I found out what you'd done. Why I wanted to run away to the furthest corner of the earth.'

To her amazement tears filled Vidal's eyes. 'Fate brought us together, *querida*,' he said softly, 'but it will be our love that keeps us together. It will be a love strong enough to withstand everything that life throws at us.'

Elena nodded. 'I'm sorry I doubted you.'

'And I'm sorry I tricked you into marriage.'

'Vidal?'

'Yes, my darling?'

'Will you make love to me?'

He needed no further asking.

CAVAN COUNTY LIBRARY

EPILOGUE

'NADIA, Angelo, come here!'

The twins ran at the sound of their father's voice. Vidal gathered them into his arms and swung them around, laughing as they squealed with delight.

Elena smiled, her heart full of joy. These last three years had fled by. Her parents had retired and were enjoying life as grandparents. She had sold her wedding-planner business to Kate, deciding, once she had discovered to her absolute terror that she was carrying twins, that she would never be able to cope. And now she was pregnant again.

She was blissfully happy. She and Vidal loved each other more than she had ever thought possible. They had their occasional ups and downs, like all couples, but the making up more than compensated.

'Don't you think you ought to be resting?' he asked her now, his silver eyes gentle on hers.

'Don't you have to go to work?'

'It can wait,' he declared with a lazy shrug.

Elena smiled. Fatherhood suited Vidal. It had changed him from a workaholic into a man who put his family first. 'I love you, Vidal Marquez,' she said softly.

He nodded. 'I love you too, my darling. With all of my heart, for the rest of my life.'

MILLS & BOON®

OCTOBER 2009 HARDBACK TITLES

ROMANCE

HISTORICAL

MEDICAL™

0909 Gen Std LP

OCTOBER 2009 LARGE PRINT TITLES

ROMANCE

The Billionaire's Bride of Convenience	Miranda Lee
Valentino's Love-Child	Lucy Monroe
Ruthless Awakening	Sara Craven
The Italian Count's Defiant Bride	Catherine George
Outback Heiress, Surprise Proposal	Margaret Way
Honeymoon with the Boss	Jessica Hart
His Princess in the Making	Melissa James
Dream Date with the Millionaire	Melissa McClone

HISTORICAL

His Reluctant Mistress	Joanna Maitland
The Earl's Forbidden Ward	Bronwyn Scott
The Rake's Inherited Courtesan	Ann Lethbridge

MEDICAL™

A Family For His Tiny Twins	Josie Metcalfe
One Night With Her Boss	Alison Roberts
Top-Notch Doc, Outback Bride	Melanie Milburne
A Baby for the Village Doctor	Abigail Gordon
The Midwife and the Single Dad	Gill Sanderson
The Playboy Firefighter's Proposal	Emily Forbes

1009 Gen Std HB

ROMANCE

Ruthless Magnate, Convenient Wife	Lynne Graham
The Prince's Chambermaid	Sharon Kendrick
The Virgin and His Majesty	Robyn Donald
Innocent Secretary...Accidentally Pregnant	Carol Marinelli
Bought: The Greek's Baby	Jennie Lucas
Powerful Italian, Penniless Housekeeper	India Grey
Count Toussaint's Pregnant Mistress	Kate Hewitt
Forgotten Mistress, Secret Love-Child	Annie West
The Boselli Bride	Susanne James
In the Tycoon's Debt	Emily McKay
The Girl from Honeysuckle Farm	Jessica Steele
One Dance with the Cowboy	Donna Alward
The Daredevil Tycoon	Barbara McMahon
Hired: Sassy Assistant	Nina Harrington
Just Married!	Cara Colter & Shirley Jump
The Italian's Forgotten Baby	Raye Morgan
The Doctor's Rebel Knight	Melanie Milburne
Greek Doctor Claims His Bride	Margaret Barker

HISTORICAL

Tall, Dark and Disreputable	Deb Marlowe
The Mistress of Hanover Square	Anne Herries
The Accidental Countess	Michelle Willingham

MEDICAL™

Posh Doc, Society Wedding	Joanna Neil
Their Baby Surprise	Jennifer Taylor
A Mother for the Italian's Twins	Margaret McDonagh
New Boss, New-Year Bride	Lucy Clark

1009 Gen Std LP

NOVEMBER 2009 LARGE PRINT TITLES

ROMANCE

The Greek Tycoon's Blackmailed Mistress	Lynne Graham
Ruthless Billionaire, Forbidden Baby	Emma Darcy
Constantine's Defiant Mistress	Sharon Kendrick
The Sheikh's Love-Child	Kate Hewitt
The Brooding Frenchman's Proposal	Rebecca Winters
His L.A. Cinderella	Trish Wylie
Dating the Rebel Tycoon	Ally Blake
Her Baby Wish	Patricia Thayer

HISTORICAL

The Notorious Mr Hurst	Louise Allen
Runaway Lady	Claire Thornton
The Wicked Lord Rasenby	Marguerite Kaye

MEDICAL™

The Surgeon She's Been Waiting For	Joanna Neil
The Baby Doctor's Bride	Jessica Matthews
The Midwife's New-found Family	Fiona McArthur
The Emergency Doctor Claims His Wife	Margaret McDonagh
The Surgeon's Special Delivery	Fiona Lowe
A Mother For His Twins	Lucy Clark

millsandboon.co.uk Community

Join Us!

The Community is the perfect place to meet and chat to kindred spirits who love books and reading as much as you do, but it's also the place to:

- **Get the inside scoop from authors about their latest books**
- **Learn how to write a romance book with advice from our editors**
- **Help us to continue publishing the best in women's fiction**
- **Share your thoughts on the books we publish**
- **Befriend other users**

Forums: Interact with each other as well as authors, editors and a whole host of other users worldwide.

Blogs: Every registered community member has their own blog to tell the world what they're up to and what's on their mind.

Book Challenge: We're aiming to read 5,000 books and have joined forces with The Reading Agency in our inaugural Book Challenge.

Profile Page: Showcase yourself and keep a record of your recent community activity.

Social Networking: We've added buttons at the end of every post to share via digg, Facebook, Google, Yahoo, technorati and de.licio.us.

www.millsandboon.co.uk

B/M&B/RTL HB

www.millsandboon.co.uk

- ◎ All the latest titles
- ◎ Free online reads
- ◎ Irresistible special offers

And there's more...

- ◎ Missed a book? Buy from our huge discounted backlist
- ◎ Sign up to our FREE monthly eNewsletter
- ◎ eBooks available now
- ◎ More about your favourite authors
- ◎ Great competitions

Make sure you visit today!

www.millsandboon.co.uk